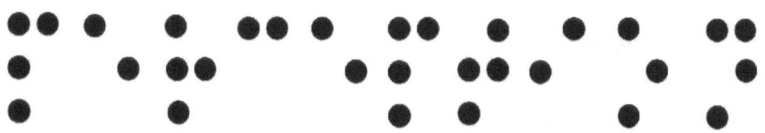

PERCEPTION

Ophelia Finsen

Also by Ophelia Finsen:

Lovers of Old Films
This is Living
Society of Lost Causes
The Women of Jimanac
Skye
The Romanian
At the Upper Villa Tyde

ISBN: 978-0-9559923-9-1

Gregory leans over the barrier and throws up. The railings are cold, chill his fingers quickly. He can feel the uneven layers of paint; cover up jobs where flakes have peeled away in the cold wind. He looks down into the dark, not sure whether the half-digested remains of his supper hit the water, or have splattered down the ship's hull. The continuous swell of water should wash any evidence away before they reach sight of land.

He feels better for a short while, but is all too aware of the lumbering nausea that has not quite vacated his stomach. The chemist had explained about the imbalance in the inner ear and sea sickness; then proceeded to refuse to sell him sea sickness tablets when he'd mentioned he'd be driving a hire car upon arrival. Being drowsy might not have been a bad thing. He could have passed out in the bar and woken as the ferry pulled into harbour. Instead, he knows he will get no sleep tonight.

Straightening, he gazes out into the deep black of the sea at night, the small twilight hours. Darkness and the sound of crashing waves. The unearthly base throb beneath him of the engines chugging, propelling the ferry ever forward. Locals in the bar calling home commented on how calm the sea was. He had fooled himself that his days of sea sickness were over – he was thirty-six this year, hardly a young stammering boy sickening over the slightest ailment. But as the ferry abandoned the sheltering coastline and pulled out into the open sea, a deep, unheard groan throbbed up from the seabed. He is glad he had enough sense not to book a cabin, for he cannot face to be inside the ship. The foot passenger ticket included a reserved 'comfortable chair' which he has not used, the chair being utterly impractical for rest and sleep. He saw who the regulars were, taking sleeping bags out of rucksacks like refugees, bedding down on the restaurant benches; soft bar seating, and any corner where they will be out of the way of passing feet.

It is bitterly cold, the wind whipping out across the open sea to attack the old, dated ferry. This is a regular journey drawing away from the main body of the country, seemingly away from everything. He looks at his watch; it's almost three in the morning. They're not due to dock in Lerwick harbour until seven.

The door from the observation deck at the back of the restaurant opens and a passenger steps out into the open-air. He walks up to the railings at the back of the vessel, takes a cigarette out of his inner jacket pocket and holds it between determined lips as he miraculously lights it, despite the wind. It is not until he has pocketed the lighter and turned to lean nonchalantly against the railings that he notices Gregory at the side of the deck.

"You out for a midnight fag as well, there?"

The man has a strong Scottish accent, weather beaten skin and a stance that suggests not even hurricane winds and tsunami waves would unsettle his balance at sea. It makes Gregory feel pathetic, not quite a man. "I don't seem to have found my sea legs."

The man smiles, nodding, as if in that sentence he has seen right through to Gregory's soul. "It takes some men a few days at a stretch at sea to find their legs," he comments, suggesting he has great sea-faring experience. He draws deeply on the cigarette. "Of course," he continues. "Some people simply aren't meant for the sea."

That would be me, Gregory thinks, and waits for the stranger to call him a big Jessie, but the insult doesn't come. The man finishes his smoke, flicks the stub away into the darkness. "Aye, well," he says, zipping up his jacket. "Only four more hours to go."

Four more hours is hardly consolation of any description. Gregory opens his mouth to make some kind of retort, but the man has already retreated into the vessel, out of the wind and the salt spray. For now, the cold fresh air seems to be the only thing keeping him alive. Gregory stays out on deck to greet the dawn, and see the southern point of mainland Shetland, Sumburgh Head, appear into view; a green, rugged terrain, virtually sparse of any human habitation from this distance. There doesn't look like there's anything to see. My God, Gregory thinks, what have I signed up for?

The ferry arrives in Lerwick, the capital town of the Shetland Islands – a small capital by international standards – at half past seven in the morning, after the fishing industry has set off, but long before the regular business of the day begins. It has been a twelve hour crossing from Aberdeen, and Gregory is overjoyed to see dry, stable land. As the ferry pulls into harbour and finally stops, he feels his body relaxing, and ventures back into the interior of the ship. Already the nausea is over, and it is soon difficult to appreciate how quick and how awful sea sickness can be. He has survived this journey, and feels bold, thinking he could conquer another trip; perhaps out to the Faroe Islands or even Iceland.

He stays onboard to eat breakfast, laughing at his new courage, knowing full well that with the first swell he would be clutching his stomach and begging for a merciful death. But with stability and a renewed hunger, he is invincible once again. Despite the lack of sleep, he is ready to get out onto the islands – his first visit to this most northerly point of the UK – and explore. But the islands aren't ready for him; it's too early in the morning.

Having looked online in advance, he knows no where will be open yet, but he cannot contain this childish excitement in the face of new discoveries. He disembarks, collecting his hold all from the luggage trolleys that have been wheeled down to the terminal building by the water side. The main building is airy and empty; a tall hollow with a number of padded seating areas, all empty of passengers. He wanders out of the main doors and up onto the main road, following it into Lerwick.

The local, family-run car hire garage he has arranged the car with won't open for another half hour. They're not far away from the ferry terminal, just a short walk down the road, past the supermarket and up to a roundabout. There are a number of bicycles for hire in the window, an old fashioned petrol pump outside of the main entrance. He double checks the opening hours before walking a little further, around to the back of the building. Here there's a car park, completely empty, overlooked by a few small shops in a red corrugated iron building. He stops by the side of a grey concrete official looking building and sets his bag on the ground. It makes a suitable seat, so he can lean back against the wall, close his eyes and bask in the sun. There is a chilly breeze, a reminder that this is far north, out in the sea. Blown apart and isolated from the rest of the world. He can feel this peace seeping into him. How blissful to be away from the rush.

When the garage opens, the process of renting a vehicle goes surprisingly quickly. A lot seems to be taken on trust and company forms signed in triplicate are not required. The rates are reasonable, which eases the pressure to find a suitable vehicle. He will only hire the car until he finds something cheap and reliable – perhaps a contradiction in terms – to buy. The girl working that Saturday morning isn't one for chat. She doesn't look that old, perhaps barely only out of her teens, and she glances uncertainly across at Gregory as he fills in the required information, not sure if she can decide whether she finds him frighteningly or unexpectedly attractive. He's clearly a lot older than she is; she guesses forties, but looking at the driving licence she sees that he's actually only in his late thirties. He spends most free time and as much working time as he can get away with in the great outdoors, regardless of the weather, and it shows in his face; an arrangement of features that revolve around the ability to crinkle up into a great smile. He has scraggy hair, growing stubble and baggy eyes after a night in the cold on the back of a ferry.

Andrew Jameson meets him at noon at the sea front in the middle of town. Gregory is admiring an old sailing ship moored into the harbour, when he hears his name; for the first time feeling like he actually belongs here, rather than just a passing tourist.

"You been waiting long?" Andrew grins as he saunters down the footpath. Andrew is an ex-pat, originally from the north of the mainland. He has since made Edinburgh his home. It has been sixteen years since he left the islands at eighteen in search of an education and hopes of a great career. In reality it has become a great education and promises of a career he doesn't intend to fill. He is, as he says his father calls him, the best educated waste of space in Scotland. He could have been a full time lecturer at the university by now, but Andrew is unable to settle, and has changed subjects and faculties. Now that he has an MA in Norwegian and a PhD in

Scandinavian Literature and a few years spent on random degree-level courses, he has decided that physics is his true calling. He is currently part way through his second PhD, working on a funded research project, which has solved his financial troubles. He does not come from a particularly rich family, yet he has managed to float by through his studies. Once the standard four years were passed and the student loans worn out, he got by on scholarships, grants and women who were prepared to put up with a lot and pay for most of it. He is a drifter who lives off other people's good nature.

"I wouldn't worry about it," Gregory tells him. "I had the car to pick up, and I've spent the morning looking around Lerwick."

Andrew snorts. "That'll have taken all of ten minutes then."

"I've had quite a walk. There's a broch up around the back..."

"Clickimin. Put a pile of rocks up and they shall come," he laughs. "Still, you'll be worrying about all that now, what with the new job. Did you say you've hired a car?"

"Yes."

"Great stuff, you can give me a lift home."

Gregory looks at him quizzically. "If I hadn't have been coming, how would you have got there?"

"Ah, something would have worked out." A statement that succinctly sums up Andrew's life.

"How long will it take us to get there?"

Andrew shrugs. "Hour and a half or so. But we're not going today."

"We're not?" Gregory sounds a little worried. He'd made no plans for staying in Lerwick.

"Don't worry, we'll go crash at David's; it's not a problem. Besides, we need to buy up some supplies before we go, and I'm not rushing back up there. It can be a bit... quiet, if you know what I mean. Anyways, we'll be off to the Lounge tonight."

"The Lounge?"

"That's the one. A good night is to be had by all. We'll worry about the rest tomorrow."

The Lounge Bar, Lerwick, has a local reputation that precedes it, and yet it does not have a dominating or pretentious look about it. It follows the same line as everything else here. It is on a small lane off the main shopping street in Lerwick – Commercial Street. This hub of retail is a relatively short, pedestrianised narrow lane hemmed in with buildings, the kind of thing that would have been built before the width of a car needed to be taken into consideration. This is the heart of the Shetlands, for there is no other major town to speak of. There is something reassuring about the small scale, the genuine atmosphere, and the understanding that this is enough. There is no need for thirty different branded glossy shops selling the same overpriced crap produced in sweat shops in the East. There is a feeling of camaraderie, of community. A sign for a local fudge shop confuses all the visitors, tourists wandering into a craft shop full of balls of wool, where a patient woman explains that the local sweets are to be found downstairs; please take the narrow ally of steps by the shop door.

The evening's outing is off up another even narrower road that pulls away from Commercial Street. A corner of the building sticks out from the natural curve of the road and progression of buildings, a painted sign above a doorway. Down between the Tourist Information and an optician's premises, it is easily missed. Even looking inside, a newcomer might be forgiven for thinking this is nothing special – the old dark wood pub tables and chairs contained within a dusky, smoky atmosphere. There is an air or tobacco and pipe smokers, even though no one is allowed to smoke inside these days. A pub that looks in need of modernising. The kind of place you'd expect to find deaf old seadogs nursing pints and not a lot else happening. Yet this is the venue to patronise, where locals come for ad hoc music sessions. There's often live music, rarely planned, but off the cuff, and at a professional standard. This is a population where folk music is ingrained in the blood, and heavily promoted at primary schools. Everyone gets a chance to play. It makes Gregory regretful; music lessons to this degree simply hadn't been available when he'd been at primary school in the north of England. And now in his mid thirties closer to forty than to thirty, it's too late to learn an instrument to be able to play this well. Anything of a lesser standard seems a waste of time.

There are three young women – anywhere from their teens to mid twenties – playing fiddles; a man on guitar accompanies them. The music is fast and furious, notes almost tripping up on one another and yet played with perfection. The fiddle music vibrates on a level that can't be heard by the human ear, and yet pulls at something in his chest. It is a comfort. Life is exciting, beautiful, a great thing to enjoy.

Andrew is setting the first round of drinks up on their table. They are a trio at present; Gregory, Andrew and Andrew's old school buddy David Henriksson. David is letting them crash for the night at his Lerwick flat, before they drive up to the Jameson homestead tomorrow. Without appearing to plan or think in advance, Andrew manages his trips home for the price of a few drinks – David will provide accommodation at Lerwick, Gregory will provide transportation back to Andrew's family home.

"Are you going up to give us a tune after these?" Gregory asks as he accepts his pint.

Andrew laughs. "I never really got into the music thing."

"He brings shame to the name Shetlander," David comments.

"Yeah." Andrew sounds distracted already, stretching up and looking across at the three fiddling blondes as they come to the end of a set of reels. "But it does mean I can get on with other things whilst you lot are all stuck up on the stage performing. Excuse me a moment."

"God Almighty," David laughs, swallowing a draught of beer. He watches Andrew approach the musicians. It looks as though they will be taking a break; especially now that some old regulars have arrived, getting accordions and well-loved fiddles out ready for a night's music. "He's not changed. Is he like this down in Edinburgh as well?"

"More or less," Gregory says. Andrew has a reputation for a weakness for a pretty face, and a short attention span. The women always hope they'll change him, deep down knowing he'll stray and eventually leave, and yet they all willingly take him on.

"And are you a student at the university as well?"

The question sounds uncertain. Whilst Andrew still has a youthful boyishness about him, Gregory definitely looks like a man, broader, weather beaten and world weary. He smiles lightly. "Not for a long time now. I'm a lecturer there."

"Oh aye," David relaxes a little with this. As if he had been worried a mature looking gent like Gregory might be a student, still living it up in the capital, sleeping around and partying. As if normal people lived that way – it wasn't just the blessed Gods of mischief like Andrew who could get away with it. And in turn if people like Gregory were still living hedonistically, there was something wrong with David, thirty-four and bored of the brainless tarts. He has a hankering for a wife these days, but would never dare to admit it when Andrew was in town. "Don't tell me you've got Andrew to tutor."

"No. We're in different departments." Thank God, Gregory thinks, tutoring Andrew would be too exhausting. "He's taken a couple of my courses in the past. I teach geography."

"Geography?" David looks confused. "I thought Andrew said you were here to write a book."

"Gents." Andrew is back at the table with two of the young women with him. "Introductions, I think. This is Sharon, a local lassie," he starts, introducing the taller of the two women, muddy blonde hair and hips starting to turn to fat. She clearly isn't the chosen girl for the night, as Andrew has his arm ever so casually draped around the shoulders of the other woman. Already feeling the spare part, Sharon is smiling, but not in her eyes; and is looking from Gregory to David and realising there will be no one special for her at this table. She is feeling every one of her twenty years.

"And this is Hafdis," Andrew continues, blind to Sharon's discomfort. "All the way from Norway."

Gregory raises his eyebrows as if Norway were the other side of the moon. It's not actually a place he has visited yet, despite the fact he has a penchant for travelling northern countries. David barely reacts. The Shetlands have a close relationship with Scandinavia; a long rich history, relatives from the Shetland bus, and these days a summer ferry connecting the islands with Norway.

"Hafdis has a hardanger fiddle," Andrew looks amazed as if fiddles are unheard of here. It sounds over done, and Hafdis is the only one not to notice. "What do you call it back home?"

"*Hardingfele*," she giggles.

"Aye, well, sit down the three of you," David says. He suddenly feels his age. Hafdis doesn't look as though she's out of her teens, and seems too young for Andrew to chase after. "Is it your first time over to Shetland, Hafdis?" he asks, trying to break up Andrew's giggling little nest.

"Oh no," Hafdis begins, her accent thick. "I have been here many times. Sharon and I are penpals since little girls."

"Well, I'm David," he says, realising Andrew has no intention of making the introductions a two-way thing. "I'm from round here. And this is Gregory. It's his first evening on Shetland, so he really is the newbie."

"Really?" Sharon is surprised that he's already found his way to the Lounge Bar. It's often overlooked by newly arrived tourists. "Did the tourist office send you here?"

Gregory is a little taken aback by her defensiveness. Already demarcating. Outsiders; locals; honorary locals. Know your place. She is a case study of youth desperate to prove a point, find a niche. She reminds him of so many of his first year students. So keen to advertise what they are to everyone they met. Broadcasting it all in the uncertainty, the instability of their delicate personalities. "Not quite; Andrew did. I'm here to work. Andrew thinks his parents will be able to rent me a basic property, a base for my work."

"You're going to be living up round Lunna?" David asks.

"Lunna?" Sharon repeats the question. Even she wouldn't want to be stuck up those narrow winding back roads. "Up with the trows."

"The what?"

David snorts into his pint. "Did Andrew not tell you about the trowies? Andrew, how could you not warn Gregory about the trowies?"

Andrew rolls his eyes. "There's no such thing."

"Oh, the sophisticated city boy now, eh? We all know there's trows up round Lunna."

"I doubt it unless you're talking about my father."

"What's all this about?" Gregory asks. "Is this the local little people?"

"Aye," David nods. "Like little trolls. You get them all over, but Lunna's supposed to be a hot spot. "Runty little buggers that come out at night to cause trouble."

"And these are definitely little trolls, not just a phenomena when the pubs are closing?"

"They're not people, as trow-like as a lot of lads are round here," Sharon says, making it sound like a joke, but there's an undertone that someone local upset her recently. "But the emptying of the pubs has probably helped the stories. The last tune we played just then was a trowie song. They're supposed to love music, and many a fiddler's heard music coming from the dark of night; a trow sitting on his mound of earth playing away. That's how we have as many folk tunes as we do here. So the stories go."

"You didn't tell me I was going to be staying with trolls," Gregory jokes.

"You may mock," Andrew says, a glint in his eye. "But you've not met my parents yet."

They leave Lerwick later than Gregory had hoped. David does not mind him waiting at the flat for Andrew to return. David is a pleasant host, but Gregory is keen to get started, to arrange his own base on the island so that the work can begin. Andrew is unreliable and Gregory worries that those promises will come to nothing; that the cottage for a low rent will prove to be little more than imagination.

Andrew eventually strolls back to the flat around noon. He has spent the night somewhere else – he never illuminates the other men on the details other than an arrogant grin, but they both assume he was with Hafdis. From what Gregory understood, Hafdis was staying with Sharon, so it can hardly have been a comfortable set up. He wonders when he grew so old, not reacting to the appeal of every young woman simply because she is young and female. Andrew still drinks this down like water, as if he is a fresh faced first year student at the university, drowning in his own hormones and desperate to spread his wild oats.

They drive the backbone of Shetland, a black line through the wilderness, connecting the small towns, villages and hamlets. It is the main road, never more than a single carriageway for each direction of traffic. It cuts through a treeless landscape of upland styled heath land, speckled with glittering lochs; lonesome farmhouses; and holiday lets; windswept rocky earth. The route swings from traversing central belts of land to sweeping by the coastline. The Shetland coast is rugged and wavering, making itself as complicated as possible and getting as much coastline as possible out of a relatively small landmass. Just before they reach Voe, Andrew tells him to take the turning marked for the Whalsay ferry and Laxo. Gregory's eyes flit across the signs pointing down single tracked roads, seemingly to nothingness; strange names, almost Scandinavian. As if this land is barely part of the British Isles. Markers of a heritage far flung from England's green fields and London's bridges.

Laxo proves to be a gathering of buildings by a junction point – he had expected a great town in the wilderness – then back out into the peace, the utter silence away from modern technology and civilisation. The sun is particularly brilliant today, the green of the regularly watered grass blazing against the cut of the blue sky. It looks like paradise to Gregory's eyes. Upon this land there is a variety of dry grassland and boggy patches; undulating hills untouched by man's design; green fields with flocks of sheep. An occasional house, reminding man has passed this way; the tarmac road a cut on the earth. They pass the ferry terminal for the Whalsay connection – terminal seeming too grand a word. Looking down to the sea, there is a small stone jetty for the landing, a modest car park by the edge with what looks like a dark wood log cabin for offices. The Shetlands are a collection of rugged islands, a network of small ferries from unassuming landing places interlinking the sparse communities. These are not servicing the masses flocking between England, France and Spain.

The road weaves around the natural topography, forcing Gregory to slow down. He hopes they will not meet much traffic coming in the opposite direction. Driving around the lower edge of a hill, the sea to their left, glittering and blue, they approach the hamlet of Lunna. The dry stone walls here grow in height, and a point where they meet at either side of the road, there are carved stone pieces on each pillar, as if to add that little touch of ceremony. You are now entering Lunna. Past a small church and graveyard; odd buildings down near the water like stone beehives; and ahead, on the brink of a hill, is a grey, imposing house, the window frames marked out in black like eyes.

"It's a hotel now," Andrew tells him.

"Oh right." Gregory glances at the building again as he takes the car up the road, swinging up the hill and around the back of the hotel. Is this to be the back-up plan when Andrew's offers falter?

"They used it in the war," Andrew continues absent minded. "It was the Shetland bus headquarters at one point. You know, the Norwegian resistance."

"I've read something about it," Gregory says vaguely. It isn't what he'd imaged, somehow not dramatic enough. The bleak and sombre countenance may be fitting but it looks too residential, too normal. Or perhaps that is the right look for a secret base fighting Nazi occupation.

"It's near here you're from?"

"Nearish," Andrew says pointing at the road ahead. "It's a dead-end road, up along the headland. We're off a side road further down here. Really cut off. Dead end." He stops talking and looks out of the passenger window, suddenly serious, stony faced. Home isn't something Andrew talks of very much. Certainly the Shetlands crop up in conversation often, but for a long time Gregory had assumed Andrew was just an enthused tourist, for he never mentioned family or people from the islands.

He leans forward before the croft track appears into view, straining against the seatbelt as if there is some force, a guiding system, pulling him back. They turn a corner and Andrew gestures at a single, rutted stoned track to the right. It is like a cut that had bled into the fields. "It's down there."

The car rattles, as if reluctant to start down the stony track. Up until this point, although winding and narrow, the roads have been in very good condition, with the added bonus of next to no traffic. It's a world away from Edinburgh city centre. Now they rumble down in-between two slight, green hills, and are soon away out of sight from the main road – if it could be called such a thing. The farmstead, the isolated place where Andrew grew up, comes into view. It is surreal that someone like Andrew comes from such a far-flung, dislocated place. Andrew thrives in the city, sophistication and people. Perhaps this starved childhood fuels the insatiable hunger. Gregory glances at the car clock. It has taken them an hour and a half to get here from Lerwick – the only real town on the Shetlands. He can image that nights are dark, cold and quiet save from the howling of the wind.

The only access track approaches the property from the back. The farmhouse is a long white building, with what looks like a kitchen garden behind. Off to the far left is the end of a squat, stone built barn. The main building is white with grey roof tiles, crenulations of yellow stone running up each corner point to define the edges of the structure. The track comes around to the front of the house where there is a gravelled yard, a tractor, car and open backed truck parked up. Further back there are a couple of sheds and a stone wall marking the perimeter. There is a metal gate with a few sheep watching through the bars.

Gregory parks up next to the truck and switches off the engine. He doesn't see the small cottage Andrew has talked about. "Is the cottage elsewhere then?"

"Oh yes," Andrew says, opening the car door. "It's away back there." He gestures vaguely in the air. "A little closer to civilisation anyway. Has a sea view and everything." He stands up out of the car, stretches, then hangs awkwardly, as if not wanting to announce their arrival. A dog barks, followed by the sound of paws on gravel as it runs across to the car, barking and sniffing at Andrew. It is a black and white border collie, not particularly aggressive or territorial – Gregory has come across some angry farm dogs in his wanderings, chained up in sheds and dreaming of a leg to bite. This dog is a little cautious of Andrew, and Gregory suspects these two have not met many times.

"Seamus!" An Irishwoman calls from the open front door. Andrew's back visibly straightens at this sound; a tightness in his face.

"Who's there?"

Gregory can't see the front door for the truck's cab, but he hears the footsteps, the pause on the threshold of the open doorway. He sees Andrew shrug awkwardly into himself. "Hello, mother."

"Hello, mother?" the woman repeats as if it is a joke. "I didn't know you were coming to visit." The dog slinks back towards the house, its head hung low as it sneaks past the matriarch and into the building.

"Thought I'd surprise you," Andrew says weakly, the mere suggestion fooling no one.

"Well, I don't know why you've come now. There's nothing doing."

He has walked into a family feud, Gregory thinks. He will have to look for alternative accommodation. If it were possible, he would have gladly sunk away, driven back towards Lerwick. He doesn't think she's realised Andrew did not arrive alone, but there's no way he can leave without her seeing. And despite her obvious cold temperament, he doesn't want to be as rude and dismissive as she had been thus far.

"How did you get here?" the woman asks.

"I came up with a colleague from the university."

"A colleague?" she sounds horrified.

That is his cue, and Gregory walks around the front of the truck, self-consciously raising a hand to say hello. The sun is shining, but there is a chill in the wind and an even worse freeze coming from this house. Andrew's mother, the Irishwoman (Gregory hadn't realised Andrew is half Irish) is a woman of distinctive eyebrows, arching over a stony gaze, her grey hair bundled up in a loose bun on the back of her head. She stands with her arms folded and is visibly horrified by Gregory's appearance.

"Good afternoon, Mrs Jameson."

"You've brought a friend here?" she continues, completely ignoring Gregory's greeting as she looks back at her first born. "What in all..." she stops, catching her tongue and regarding Gregory as a conscious person for the first time. "*An bhfuil Gaeilge agat?*"

The question is directed at Gregory – he can tell it is a question from the upward lilt at the end and the pause, impatient and seething, waiting for an answer. Beyond that he knows nothing, assuming its Gaelic she's speaking. He opens his mouth, unsure what to say, not even certain if a response in English would be appropriate at this moment.

"*Cén fáth a raibh tú a thabhairt air anseo?*"

Andrew sighs, as loud as a stage sigh. "Mother, I have come to visit, and Gregory's come to Shetland to work..."

"Andrew!" she interrupts him, shaking the tea towel she is holding by her side like a whip. She isn't interested in the details. "*Tú riamh smaoineamh*! I suppose you'll both be wanting supper."

"I don't want to put you to any inconvenience." Gregory says.

"You two might as well go into the parlour," Mrs Jameson says, looking at neither of them as she marches out of the house. "I'll have to get some more potatoes," she adds, heading the direction of the barn.

Andrew stuffs his hands into his pockets, physically relaxing as his mother leaves. A touch of his nonchalance is back. "Come on then," he says to Gregory. "Better do what she says and go inside."

"I'm getting the impression no one knew we were coming."

"She likes surprises."

"It didn't look like that. Have you led me on a wild goose chase?"

"Don't worry about it," Andrew reassures him. "Mother's just a bit direct. Probably going through the change, you know what I mean? Come on into the house. The worst is over." And with that unconvincing promise, he leads the way into his old childhood home.

The parlour – an antiquated description already foreboding – is not a comfortable room. The sun has gone in behind clouds and the light is grey and dismal. But it is not so much the lighting conditions as the decor and the general atmosphere that makes it near stifling.

Andrew cannot settle, and is barely sitting before he is back on his feet, stalking the room and itching to leave. "I'll have to speak to Pa as soon as he gets in," Andrew says. "Get this cottage sorted out."

"I don't know whether that's such a good idea," Gregory tells him. He has already drawn up a mental list of people he can call on for a temporary stop gap. Although he has never been to the Shetlands before, he has a few colleagues and contacts here: people who have moved up here for work; others that he has been in touch with before via email and the phone when working on projects.

There's the bird station at Sumburgh Head; and at a push even the one on Fair Isle. He could go to one of those and get some help getting established.

"I've said you can stay there, and I'll get it sorted," Andrew is glowering out of the window. "Don't mind her. Pa is all right."

"Right." Gregory looks uncertainly around the parlour. This is a fine start to his sabbatical – not exactly what he had hoped for. Sitting in a Victorian psychopath's parlour – for that is what it feels like, with the antique, dark wood imposing dresser, glass display cabinets of dusty taxidermy and a prominent crucifix suspended on the wall. Every inanimate object in that room sits in judgement of its occupants.

Dinner, served in a proper dining room, is not a lot better. Andrew's father, John Jameson, a lean, red-faced, weather-hardened Scot, sits at the head of the table. There is a moment of surprise on his face when he sees Gregory, a question of who and why, but he does not verbalise it, instead choosing to silently wait for the facts to reveal themselves. He moves himself into the dining room, having just washed his hands in the kitchen; not a word to his wife or his son, despite the fact that it must have been some time since he last saw Andrew. It is strained, as if no one wants to be here, but they're all too stubborn, determined, and will be damned if they are to be the first to give way.

In the end, it is Andrew's mother, Eilidh, who speaks first. In anyone else it would have been an admission of weakness, but she immediately takes control. "Will you be staying long, Andrew?" she asks as she spoons more boiled potatoes onto her plate.

"Just a few days."

"Have you seen your sister?"

Andrew almost inhales the peas on his fork.

Eilidh arches her eyebrows very casually. "Shea's supposed to be coming back to the farm tomorrow."

"Shea." Andrew's tone is flat. He doesn't sound impressed.

"That is her name," his mother says primly.

It ought not to be surprising that Andrew has siblings. He had said nothing of his home since Gregory has known him, so of course a sister would fall into this unmentioned realm. "Do you have many siblings?"

Andrew glances at his mother. "Shea's my baby sister," he finally says. "She goes to school in Lerwick, so she doesn't live up here full time."

A baby sister still in full time education. Gregory carefully sets his knife and fork down. That would make a big age difference between Andrew and his sister. Judging from the silence; that definite sense of separation between husband and wife, he can imagine Eilidh doesn't give John Jameson many opportunities for increasing the family. Perhaps this isolated farm life has ground her down over the years.

An uncomfortable silence follows. Clearly Andrew's disinterest in talking about his home life stems from his parent's attitude on the matter. No one appears to want to acknowledge why they're sitting around the table together. Eilidh laces her fingers together and looks over to Gregory. "You've not told us why you've come to Shetland, Mr Hughson," she begins, changing the subject. "Are you here as a tourist or because my son needed someone to pay for his ferry ticket?"

Gregory ignores the dig at her child, not wanting to get drawn into an age-old family argument. Although Andrew neither contributed to the petrol nor the car hire, he did at least pay for his own ferry ticket, and has made determined promises of arranging cheap accommodation for him. "I'm actually here for work," Gregory says. "I work at the University of Edinburgh, but I'm on my sabbatical."

"I thought sabbaticals were when you academics locked yourself away to write books."

"I will be doing that in a way."

"And what department do you work in? Not Norwegian, I hope."

"Geography."

"So you've come to write a book on the geography of the Shetlands?"

"Of a sort. It's a commission between the tourist board, the Scottish Arts Council and my publishers. There's a lack of a good book on the Shetlands in print at the moment. It's to be a definitive guide: history, geography, culture, the people, the wildlife; with information on walking trails, places of interest, and the usual lists of hotels, self catering and campsites."

"It sounds like a big ask for one man on a sabbatical year. You must come to the Shetlands often."

"This is actually my first visit. I've got a year and an editor who'll make sure I'm keeping to the straight and narrow."

"So you'll have to travel around Shetland."

"Yes. I'm also working on a research project for the RSBP, to do with the red-necked phalarope..." he falters, glancing from one blank face to the other, not sure if they're bored or have no idea what he's talking about. "It's a little wading bird. A migrant, but very rare in the UK. The Shetlands is one of the few places where it breeds, but even here it's very localised. I think Fetlar has one of the strongholds, if that's what it can be called."

"Oh yes," Eilidh seems pleased about this. "Fetlar's one of the northern isles. You'd have to go up to the north and get the ferry over to Yell first, and then another to Fetlar. I suppose you'll be basing yourself up there, to watch these wee birds and write your book."

"Come off it," Andrew mutters. "You don't have to go all the way to Fetlar to see those birds. We've had a pair breeding on the wee loch on the farm as long back as I can remember."

Eilidh's eyes flash at Andrew.

"I'll show you, tomorrow," Andrew tells Gregory.

"I don't think Mr Hughson will have time," she says tightly. "He'll have a fair journey to get to Fetlar, and a lot to organise, I shouldn't imagine, if he's to be living there."

"He's not staying up there," Andrew retorts, Gregory now forgotten in this battle between mother and son. "I've said he can stay in the wee croft down the far end of the farm."

Eilidh's cutlery clatters on her plate. She is furious that another has assumed they can take liberties over her home. The colour fades from her lips; they are so tightly pressed together. "It's out of the question. That place is not fit for a pig." She regards Gregory. "I'm afraid my son has misled you. You'll have to make alternative arrangements."

"Mother!"

"Don't you *mother* me. It's not your decision, and you shouldn't be suggesting such a wreck as accommodation to university staff." She paused, as if about to compromise. "This may affect your plans.

You can stay here tonight. It'll be too late to try and find somewhere now."

This is the last thing Gregory wants. He would rather sleep in the car, but he can hardly say this to Andrew's family, and wouldn't wish to suffer the consequences of Eilidh's temper, should such a suggestion be made. But he is prepared to give her a way out; happy to pay for it himself if it means he can flee this tension. "That's kind of you but I don't want to put you to any trouble. I think there's a guesthouse in Lunna; Andrew pointed the building out when we drove through."

Eilidh is staring at her son. "No, you can stay here tonight." It is not so much of an offer as a command.

Eilidh shows Gregory his room directly after dinner, then disappears into the kitchen for the rest of the evening. Andrew has already retreated to his childhood bedroom, and Gregory finds he is alone, mentally cursing Andrew for having brought him up here. He must have known this was the way his mother would react.

He has collected his rucksack from the car, and is entering the main corridor of the house again when he bumps into Andrew's silent father, John Jameson. He nods to Gregory, who in turn wonders if the man must be a mute, for he has yet to hear the farmer utter a single word; when John takes him to one side for a chat.

"Andrew said you were wanting to stay in the wee croft."

So many words at once are a surprise. Calm, rational, with no game playing in his expression. Gregory is a little taken aback, for a moment speechless. "Andrew had suggested it, but it's not a problem, I have a few contacts..."

"Eilidh's right, it is run down," John continues, ignoring Gregory's polite soundings about alternative accommodation. "And it will always be a bit basic you understand. No hot water. But I could get a water supply to it. I could get it set up if you could give me a week. This place to stay, would it be for your year off?"

"For most of it."

"And you'd be looking to rent it?"

Gregory feels they've gotten down to the burning issue now. "Well, yes, of course. The funding allows for this for my work. We're not looking to take advantage of anyone."

"The farm doesn't make as much as it used to, you see." John explains. "And the extra cash would help."

"Would this not cause a problem with Mrs Jameson?"

"Don't mind Eilidh, she's just a wee bit hot headed. If you can give me a week to get it sorted out, the croft is yours. I'm sure we can agree on a rent. The cottage's not here at the farm, but a bit down the road, closer to Lunna. You'll be able to come and go as you please, go study those birds and plan your walking trails."

Gregory isn't sure that he'll be able to get as a good an offer on such short notice. "I've got to go touch base with colleagues at Sumburgh. I could get that done, then come back in a week and we can sort out the finer details. I won't always be at the cottage, as I will have to travel around the islands, but I will be needing a permanent base I can come and go from."

John appears pleased with this arrangement. "That will be grand. A week tomorrow we'll meet again and you can see your cottage."

Later that night, Gregory admits to himself that he's embroiled himself in committing to this cottage – John looked as though it was a done deal, and has probably already mentally spent the rent on the farm. He will be trapped in the side lines of Andrew's family feuding for the next year. He hopes the cottage is a long way from the main farm buildings, and he will barely have to see the Jamesons whilst he is here. Hopefully the residents of Lunna are amicable folk, and he will slip into a more welcoming community there. For whilst Gregory is a lone wolf, happy to work independently, he does know from past experience, that solitude on these projects can drive a man mad.

It is almost eleven at night, and the household has retired to bed. The silent farming life, ink black night outside – perhaps there is nothing else to do but sleep and wait for the next rise of the sun. Gregory is still awake, sat on top of the covers of the bed, legs stretched over the hard mattress, eyes flicking between the austere crucifix on the wall and the notebook he is flicking through. One week before he has his base. He needs to go down to Sumburgh Head, the most southerly point of the Shetland mainland, to touch base with the bird centre there, and his contact for the phalarope project. Then there's an old university colleague who is now working on the bird station on Fair Isle. He ought to be able to scrounge somewhere to stay on the two visits, and it ought to fill in the week admirably. He just needs to call them to forewarn them –

or would it be better to arrive unexpected? Give them no opportunity to put him off.

He puts the notebook down and leans his head against the cream-painted wall; listens to the wind blow outside. Although there are hills here, and an expanse of land, they are out on a limb, on a rugged spit of land, and there is no shelter from the North Sea gales aside from the topography of the land. There are no trees to provide any cover, as Shetland is well-known for. The wind buffets against the farmhouse walls, whirs against the windows. There is something comforting in feeling proof against the weather – rain or wind outside, but the sturdy stone building will not bend, and inside there is shelter.

There is a crunch of gravel outside, which he thinks nothing of, until it is followed by five or six equal crunches in a steady beat. The noise of the wind appears to drop, and the silence in his room increases, if such a thing is possible. He finds himself focusing on the sound outside. There is a pause, then slower crunches. Each crunch like a footstep. He had assumed that everyone was asleep in bed, Seamus the dog curled up in his basket in the kitchen. Although these steps sound too heavy for the paws of a dog. Perhaps it is a sheep loose of the fields.

Slow calculated crunches. Then nothing. He is concentrating solely on the sound, although annoyed by it. Like a sleepless wreck listening to a snoring sleeper, unable to relax in that pause before the next grunt comes out. He realises he is tense, almost nervous, of the fact that there is someone or something stood in the yard outside his window, where all the vehicles are parked in a line.

Gregory puts one foot on the floor, intending to go to the window, somewhat apprehensively, and look outside. He steps to the window, touching the curtains, almost not daring to peek outside, but expecting something, a great unknown to be standing and staring back at him.

There is nothing. The moon is out, and after a moment of squinting, his eyes adjust, and he can see the yard, the barn and sheds surrounding the area. The vehicles are parked unharmed, including his hire car. But there are no people, no sheep – nothing, not even a dog or a farm cat skulking out in the night. Gregory pulls the curtains to, shaking his head at his own foolishness. The atmosphere of this place and this dysfunctional family has already got to him. He will be glad when the cottage is ready and he will not have to stay here, or impose on friends anymore.

Andrew looks tired the next morning, baggy-eyed and wan, as if he has barely slept. He is late out of bed. He stumbles from the house after Gregory has already eaten a silent breakfast with the matriarch. Gregory is propped against the bonnet of his hire car, having just spoken to his colleague at Sumburgh head. He is surprised that he managed to get mobile phone reception up here – it was down to one bar inside the farmhouse, but the yard itself appears to be a bit of a hotspot.

"Sleep well?"

Gregory turns at the sound of crunches sifting gravel – definitely human footsteps – and watches Andrew approach. "Reasonable. Not as well as you look though," he adds sarcastically. "Was it you I heard roaming about outside late last night?"

"I took to my bed early," Andrew mutters, before glancing at Gregory and seemingly waking up. "What? Roaming about? Maybe it was me." He is vague, gazing over to the gate where the sheep peer through the bars in curiosity.

Gregory can't help but laugh. This is worse than one of Andrew's partying hangovers, yet the man must be stone cold sober. "You having withdrawal symptoms? Can you not remember? Or are you a bit of a sleepwalker."

Andrew doesn't meet his eye. "Something like that. So, what news?"

He looks down at the phone in his hand. "I've just been on the phone to a couple of colleagues I need to go and see. Alan's actually on the mainland right now, he won't be landing in Lerwick again till Thursday; said I can go over to Fair Isle with him. And I've spoken to Sumburgh Head. My contact there said they've a student leaving today, so I could have their room as of tomorrow for a couple of nights. In a lighthouse."

"Christ." Andrew raises his eyes.

"Your father caught me last night," Gregory continues. "Said he'll do up this cottage for me and I can have it in a week's time."

"Are you going to take it?"

"Well, yes, it'll be a bit basic, but it's cheap and it's out of the way. I can knuckle down and get my work done without distractions."

"I don't know if it was such a good idea."

"What, the cottage? You suggested it in the first place."

"I know, but I've not been back here for a few years. You forget..." he drifts off, surveying the yard. "No, forget it. It's just family issues, and you won't be staying on the farm. The croft is a good healthy distance from here. With luck you'll never see any of them again. So you say you've got a place to stay as of tomorrow night?"

"Yes, so we can head off back to Lerwick today if you like. Or I can leave you here for more family time. I'm not actually sure how long you were planning on staying." Gregory pauses, expecting a response, but Andrew is just staring out at the horizon. "I can stop in a hotel in Lerwick tonight. Although it'd be good if you could show me where you've seen the phalaropes on the farm."

"I should stay a bit longer," Andrew says. "I've not been here for ages. Tell you want, stay another night, then you can give us a lift back into town tomorrow."

"I don't want to put your mother to any trouble."

"No trouble at all." He brightens, a light at the end of the tunnel and the thought of Lerwick, then the ferry and train, a few days' recovery time back in Edinburgh, the Shetlands will all but forgotten again. "Come on, let's take a stroll; go find those bloody birds."

Andrew leads the way onto the family farmland, cutting across small stonewall-lined fields and up onto wilder terrain, with deep heather scrubland, undulating hills and a sea wind that they have to lean into as they walk. Andrew stumbles onto a narrow pathway through the heather, probably a sheep track that they follow with nothing better to choose from. Gregory realises that Andrew isn't sure where he is going; probably has no idea where the phalarope's are – if indeed he has ever seen them on this part of the island. They reach a small loch, stumbling out of the heather and onto the pebble-strewn shoreline. Andrew stands with his hands on his hips, announcing loudly that he's found 'it', in the process scaring away anything that might have been there. Gregory is not going to see any wildlife whilst Andrew is with him.

Gregory drops down into a heather bush, feeling the branches scratch up the back of his jacket. He sticks out his legs like neat pins, the heels of his boots kicking into the earth, marking his place. There's a small, reddish-brown feather caught up in the grass close to the water. He picks it up and turns it over in his fingers. He is not that good on birds' feathers, certainly not enough to positively say which species dropped this. It's small enough to have come from one of these small illusive wading birds; but likewise it could be from something else.

"You'll survive another night on the farm?"

"What?" Gregory looks up, pocketing the feather.

"I know it's a bit grim."

"This is why you rarely come to visit?"

Andrew doesn't answer, but turns back to the lake, only a corner of his face visible to Gregory. "We're not what you'd call a close family."

Not in the slightest, Gregory agrees. He doesn't quite understand why they continue with this feeble pretence that they are a family, living together, keeping in touch, if barely. It's clear they do not enjoy being in one another's company. Perhaps he is just spoilt in his own roots, and most families are like the Jamesons. Maybe he has not appreciated how lucky he is for the simple fact that he gets along with his family. There are more distant relations that he does not particularly care for, but in the main there is no animosity.

"I'll head down to Sumburgh tomorrow," Gregory adds, cursing the fact that he's been persuaded to stay another night for no good reason, too soft to say no to leaving Andrew to find an alternative route back to Lerwick. "I'll give you a lift back into town."

"Good man."

The sun is particularly strong, the sky an immense blue. Despite the wind, it feels warm. Gregory stands up. "I'm going to walk up around the headland," he tells Andrew. "See what's doing."

Andrew makes a move to follow him as he starts up around the edge of the loch, then changes his mind, realising he knows nothing of the farm to show Gregory. He will probably discover more on his own. Gregory seems a little disgruntled that he's not able to get away sooner – twenty four hours and already he wants to flee the Jameson family. Andrew can understand this. He heads back towards the farm, planning to side track it and head into Lunna, get a wee drink at the bar in the guesthouse.

Seamus is waiting by the gate when Gregory strides back that afternoon. Already a familiar, the dog doesn't bark, but watches eagerly as he opens the gate, slipping into the farmyard. He pads up to Gregory, who in turn gives him an absent-minded ruffle around the scruff of the neck.

Gregory heads over to the hire car, unlocking the boot and riffling through the contents, certain there was a bag of apples somewhere. He is quite hungry, but disinclined to go into the Jameson household and beg food. He wonders if the guesthouse they drove past on the way here serves food.

"Who the fuck are you?"

Having found the apples, his hand hovers, surprised both by the tone; the suddenness of the question, and the voice itself. It is not a voice he has come across before: surly, Scottish, young and female. More direct and unwelcoming than even Eilidh would dare to be.

Gregory is not keen on teenagers. Professionally he has to put up with his share of seventeen and eighteen year olds starting university. Very few want to do any work or commit to anything more than accepting the massive loans and staying out all night. One of the many perks of the sabbatical ought to be that he doesn't have to deal with youth and *the attitude*. Disinclined to bow down to rudeness, he takes his time, choosing an apple from the bag, and lowering the car boot before deigning to acknowledge the question.

Before the car stands a teenager. She has bleach-blonde hair tied up in scruffy pig tails, heavy eye makeup and garish lipstick. She could be anywhere between the ages of fourteen and twenty two. Dressed in skinny jeans, short top and jacket, a sliver of midriff exposed to the Shetland wind, she continues to stare unapologetically at Gregory; her stance an odd mixture of aggression, distaste and provocative teasing. She looks like a clichéd rebel, a Lolita for the new age, with pierced ears and eyebrow, a selection of heavy cheap rings on her fingers, and doubtless tattoos hidden on her body.

"I could ask you the same question."

This irritates her, and her mouth tightens childishly, as if she is about to stick out her bottom lip in a sulk. "I live here."

"You must be Shea," Gregory responds. "You weren't here yesterday, but your mother mentioned you."

She laughs coldly at this. "That would be a first, then, wouldn't it? You've still not said who you are."

"I'm going to be renting a wee cottage from your father."

"A wee cottage? You mean the old croft? That old shithole. How would you know about that anyway? It's not up for rent; no one in their right mind would pay money to go in there."

"It was your brother's suggestion."

"Andrew?" She is very unimpressed by the mention of his name. "Christ, is that arsehole here as well? I should have stayed in town." She stops, assessing Gregory again. He does look older than Andrew; perhaps he is twice her age. He looks like a proper weathered man, different to the usual boy-men she takes, but she must consider all opportunities. If he knows Andrew, he may be an academic. He may have money. She is still very sheltered from the world, with a poor comprehension of the hierarchy of professions and who earns the real money back on the mainland. "Are you from the university then? Is that how you know Andrew?"

"Hey, Gregory!" Andrew's voice cuts into their conversation. Andrew is strolling up the road to the farm, comfortably intoxicated and ready to meet his family head on. He sees Shea, in her usual stance, legs akimbo like a sharp shooter. Christ, he hopes she isn't eyeing up Gregory as the next potential shag. People back in Edinburgh call him promiscuous, but he is nothing on Shea, and she's barely seventeen. "Just ignore her."

"Hey Gregory," Shea mimics in a whinny, nasal voice, scowling at Andrew as he approaches. "Have you brought your boyfriend to meet the olds?"

"Shut your face, you wee tart," he says, and with that sentence, disregards her completely. These have been the first words they have exchanged for over two years. "I've just been at the guesthouse," he continues, speaking to Gregory as though Shea isn't there at all. "They're serving food tonight. Shall we stroll on down and give mother a rest? I'll introduce you round to a few folks; might as well as you're going to be staying here."

"Sure. Do you want to drive down or shall we walk?"

"Walk, then we don't have to think about what we drink." Andrew turns on his heel, perfectly content to walk back to the village immediately.

"You two off on a date?" Shea sneers as the two men leave her, heading down the farm road.

Neither respond, and Andrew scowls at the scenery. "Fuck me; I'll be glad when I'm back in Edinburgh."

It is surprising how many people are at the bar that evening. It appears to be a sparsely populated landscape and yet heads bob up at regular intervals, multiplying like friendly bacteria. He meets more people that evening than he can visually identify as living on the same street back in Edinburgh. The farmers, the fish farmers, fishermen, gas installation workers, guesthouse staff and a couple of tourists gather in the bar, chatting in a friendly, inoffensive way to Andrew and Gregory. Here it feels as though they are on an even footing, for although Andrew is technically a local, it has been so long since he last lived here, he is little more than a memory, and now only passing through. A trip down memory lane. Gregory, who is to be in the area for several months, proves to be of greater interest.

There is some general surprise when Andrew mentions that Gregory will be staying on the old croft. The farmers say it could be made habitable reasonably quickly, if one does not require too many creature comforts. The women shake their heads and mutter that in this day and age, they wouldn't want to have to do without hot water. There is some reference to the Jameson family, an awkward comment that Shea has gone a little wild. Gregory gets the impression that the Jamesons are loners, at least here at Lunna – from the hints he guesses Shea isn't often alone in Lerwick – and John and Eilidh are rarely, if ever seen in the village to socialise. Sheep farming is a very tying profession, they say, long hours and low pay. And when Eilidh is not looking after the farmhouse, she is in Lerwick working at the day job. She is a midwife, something which surprises Gregory as she does not seem to have the right temperament to work in a caring, sensitive role within the health service. Or perhaps it is just what is needed, for surely no baby would dare be late or cause trouble on the way out if they knew that Eilidh was waiting impatiently at the end to receive them into the world.

They drink and chat late into the night, and as the talk is doused in high proof volumes, the subject of the trowies finds its way back to the table. There are the usual line of jokes and half-baked stories of the little folk that live around Lunna; whose fiddle music can be heard late at night; who appear when the mists collect over the land, and will turn up to scare and cause mischief.

By two in the morning the population in the bar is sparse and the landlord decides to call it a night. Andrew and Gregory leave the grey, thick walls of Lunna House, proof against all weathers, all disasters and time, and begin the long walk along the single track tarmac road to the farm. They have a torch each, the beams flashing here and there erratically, but there is also moonlight from a half moon. The wind whips over the island, but they are reasonably sheltered by the low hills, and warmed and numbed by the alcohol in their veins.

When they get back to the farm, Andrew heads straight off to bed like a naughty boy sneaking back after an illicit night out. Gregory remains in the chill night, propped against the side of his car, torchlight shining down at his feet and his eyes to the sky. There is virtually no artificial light here, aside from the hall light Andrew has left on. The depth and the immensity of the night sky are impressive; a complex network of sprinkled stars overhead. He cannot remember the last time he had such a good view of the sky at night.

He walks across the farm yard to the gate to the fields and the land beyond. His footsteps crunch against the gravel, and he smiles to himself, recalling the silly nervousness of last night when he had thought he'd heard someone creeping about outside. At the gate he puts one foot on the lowest rung, and leans into both the gate and the wind, watching the expanse of the stars.

When the sun has gone down, it is difficult to judge distances. Lights appear as blobs on the black, with no points of reference to place them in context. In his drunkenness, Gregory doesn't immediately react to the light somewhere out in the fields or the moorland ahead, swinging from side to side like a lantern. His eyes focus on the yellowed light; the smile wilts on his lips. There is a burning flame, a light in a lantern, or perhaps a torch, blowing side to side on the hills. For a moment he wonders if it's something John has set up on a pole for some farming-related reason. A night light for the sheep. But no, this light is not fixed, it is moving; or to be more exact, it is being carried.

He leans back from the gate, his fingers still locked around the top rung. His mouth is dry, his tongue sticking to the roof of his mouth. What is this? It's past three in the morning and everyone is in the house. Asleep. He looks back to the farmhouse, to the comforting static light from the bulb in the front entrance. Perhaps it is John out in the fields, tending to a sick sheep. Somehow he cannot convince himself of this explanation. He cannot be sure if the light is coming towards him or heading away, but an irrational terror in the pit of his stomach pushes him away from the gate and back to the house. He does not want to know. Something is not right.

Gregory hurries into the hallway and shuts the front door. There is a keyhole, but no keys – the Jamesons never lock the house – and no way to keep the night outside. He spots a bolt at the top of the door, and quickly pushes it into place. Staggering backwards, he slumps down upon the steps, like a child waiting for the return of a parent, and watches the front door. He knows that he should stop being dramatic, turn off the light and go up to bed. But he cannot help himself.

For a good time, nothing happens. Gregory's pulse drops a little, and he relaxes. He is ready to quit this silly game of scaring himself, and go up to bed, when there is a sound outside the house. He watches as the front door handle is turned downward. The door is pushed, yet the bolt holds true, and whoever, whatever, is on the other side of the door cannot enter. Gregory waits for the voice of John Jameson to tell whichever fool locked the door to let him back in, for he can see the hall light is on and he knows someone is there. But no words are spoken. The door handle is released, suddenly springing back up into position. The sound of movement retreating away from the door.

An awful thought strikes him – are there any other entrances into the farmhouse? He ought to check; he ought to look out of the window and see who is walking away, rather than cowering on the stairs like a little girl. But he cannot help himself. He turns out the light and hurries upstairs, careful to prop a chair up under the handle of his bedroom door.

Anna-Mary Walsh is a jovial, laughing woman. Her rounded face is shaped liked sunshine, with shoulder length hair the beams of light, forever coming free of hair slides and ties, twisting loose in the wind and tangling. She is the head warden at the bird station at Sumburgh Head – a steep hill balanced on the very southern tip of the Shetland mainland. The lighthouse stands at the peak with its metre-thick walls embedded into the towering rocky outcrop. The edges of land are rugged, as if the sea has taken great bites out of the earth, leaving torn, bare rock faces, treacherous cliffs smashing into the broiling sea below. Almost defying gravity, seabirds settle themselves and their eggs upon every slight crevice and rock shelf, the screams of kittiwakes and guillemots cutting through the fresh salty air. Higher up where the grassy slopes cling, puffins make their homes in vacated rabbit burrows, their comical faces calmly watching the tourists in waterproof jackets coo over them for a couple of minutes before moving on.

"We had a pod of killer whales passing by yesterday," Anna-Mary continues as she slurps her tea. "I'll take you out in a mo; show you the good points for watching for them."

There is a quiet snort of amusement from the other side of the office. "Yeah, anywhere where there's water."

Anna-Mary raises her eyebrows. She is a laid back, reasonable boss, and doesn't take any particular offence. She knows that there is no malice intended, and besides, Astrid has worked very hard the six months she has been with the bird station. "Did I introduce you to our student?" she asks Gregory, and they both look over to the short, blonde woman hunkered down behind her computer. She looks like a little doll, barely out of her teens and not built for island weather. But Astrid has Viking blood in her veins and has yet to find anything on the Shetlands beyond her.

"Are you the student working on the phalarope project?"

She shakes her head. "I'm monitoring kittiwake populations here and on Fair Isle."

"I'll get you Ivan's number," Anna-Mary adds. "He's working on that project as part of his degree. He's living up on Fetlar. You're not basing yourself there?"

"No. I need to get about to all the islands for my other job. I'll be based on the mainland. I've got a cheap basic cottage that should be ready by the end of the week."

"Right, the cottage. Where did you say it was again?"

"Lunna."

"Lunna? It's trow country up there, you know?"

Gregory smiles. "I've been told this."

"They'll be fine as long as you let them be," Anna-Mary jokes. "Have you heard any strange music late at night? They tend to come out and sit on hillocks playing the fiddle."

"No music, but last night..." he falters, the words spoken before he realises what he is admitting to. He does not want to discuss last night with anyone. He is ashamed to think that he was actually scared, his imagination fuelled by the alcohol, the wee small hours and the unknown behind the door. No one mentioned the locked door the next day, but on reflection, Gregory is sure it must have been John Jameson returning from tending to one of the sheep. He probably assumed Gregory or Andrew locked the door in ignorance – these city slickers coming from the land of thieves and mistrust.

The 'but' has been put out in the open. Astrid, whose typing slowed during their conversation, is no longer making any pretence that she is working, and has pushed her chair back from the computer terminal so that she can watch both Anna-Mary and Gregory. Even Anna-Mary puts down her mug of tea. "You can't just leave a comment like that hanging there," she tells Gregory.

"Ah, no. It seems very silly in the cold light of day."

"Doesn't matter."

"I should stress this was when I was coming back from the bar."

"As all good trowie sightings are," Astrid says.

"It was probably just John coming back from the fields in the dark," Gregory continues, needing to offer up as many excuses as he can for what he is about to say. "I'd just stayed outside the house a moment or two to look at the sky. And I saw this light out in the fields or on the moorland – it's a bit hard to say because away from the house it was pitch dark. It was just a little light, moving, as though someone was carrying it."

Anna-Mary looks bored with the story already. "Trows off to a party? Who knows."

"Either that or a will-o'-the-wisp," Astrid mutters.

"Sorry, what was that?" Anna-Mary laughs. "Did you just mention a chocolate bar?"

"I said will-o'-the-wisp," Astrid speaks more clearly this time. "It's a little light, supposedly moving, that's seen at night in the countryside, places such as bogs and moors. These days they reckon it's just gases coming out of bogs that spontaneously combust when coming into contact with air. But people used to have all kinds of stories for what they were. Little imps or fairies trying to tempt travellers off the right track. The souls of people too wicked to get into heaven but too good for hell, who are forced to walk the earth for eternity. It can even be the souls of dead children; they're trapped here by mischief or the fact they died too young. I remember one about a girl who had gone out to gather herbs on the Sabbath so she'd be ready to start work the next day. She was warned not to work on a Sunday, but went anyway and was never seen again. A bobbing light, like a light held within ribs was seen in the area where she disappeared after that."

"Astrid has two main interests," Anna-Mary tells Gregory. "Natural history and folklore. Whose farm are you staying on?"

"The Jameson farm. I know Andrew from Edinburgh. He arranged the cheap rental for me."

"Andrew Jameson," Anna-Mary mulls over the name. "Oh yes, I know him. Or rather I did know him. Christ, he's been gone from the islands a good long time now. I was in his class at school. I'm not surprised he fled to the mainland. His parents aren't exactly what you'd call sociable."

"There's certainly an atmosphere."

"You actually stayed on the farm?"

"Had to; the cottage needs doing up."

"Jesus Christ," Anna-Mary bursts out, perhaps a little excessive for the lack of social niceties one can expect from the Jamesons.

"That's bloody creepy. I've only just remembered." She looks over at Astrid. "That willo wispa you were talking about. I wonder if it's Andrew's dead little sister you've seen."

"Andrew's little sister?" Gregory laughs. "I met her yesterday and she is very much alive."

"Yeah, Shea's not dead," Astrid agrees. "I don't really know her; she was a few years below me at school; but her reputation precedes her. Everyone's heard of Shea Jameson. She's the high school slut."

"No, I don't mean her. This happened back in primary school. Andrew had a younger sister, couple of years below him. I can't remember what she was called. Inge or Alison or something. She died; she can only have been seven or eight. I remember it, suddenly she just stopped coming to school."

"I had no idea. Andrew's never mentioned another sister." Although Andrew never speaks about family, be they alive or dead, Gregory thinks.

"I don't suppose it's something they like to talk about. Maybe explains why they're the way they are."

A week can go frighteningly quickly, Gregory reflects as he drives north from Lerwick. He is alone for the first time on Shetland, and already the roads and the landscape hold a certain familiarity, as though he has been here for months rather than weeks. He is already materially a local, driving his own car rather than a rental. It's just a cheap old banger, but it ought to see the year out. The car is his, local number plate and everything. This past week has been a pleasant introduction to the island; a chance to catch up with old colleagues on Fair Isle, meet various contacts for the year ahead. His new colleagues are down-to-earth, decent folk, although Anna-Mary's persistence in constant companionship as though he would swiftly pine away from solitude wears a little thin by the end of his stay at Sumburgh.

Although he is not particularly looking forward to seeing the Jamesons again, he is eager to see the cottage, imagining a rustic idyll. More importantly he is anticipating enjoying the peace of his own space. He can keep the bulk of his gear in one place, and not constantly feel like an over-burdened tourist on the move. It will be somewhere to truly enjoy the tranquillity of the Shetlands, shut the door against the crowds, and get down to some work.

John Jameson is unloading a small collection of mismatched cardboard boxes from the back of his truck when Gregory pulls into the farmyard. He walks across as the car comes to a standstill, hunching forward as the driver's window is rolled down. "Afternoon," he starts. "I thought I'd be seeing you sometime soon, so I've been hanging around the farm."

Gregory isn't sure whether this is an idle comment or a loaded insinuation of time wasting, but as John Jameson will be earning rent money from this transaction, he ignores any undertones. "Is it far from here?"

"Edge of our farm. We're best off taking your car straight down there. I can walk back; got a couple of sheep on the way I want to take a look at. I can catch a ride with you?" He doesn't wait for an answer, letting himself into the passenger seat beside Gregory.

"Which way now?"

"Back down to the main road, then turn left for the village."

By 'main road', Gregory assumes John means the single-line tarmac road off which this rough farm track diverts.

Shortly before they reach the village, the grey rectangular vision of the old WWII resistance headquarters looming into view on the horizon, John tells him to take a turning to the left. It's barely a turning, grass ruts taking advantage in the break in stone walling. Gregory takes the car slowly up the green lane, thinking this is going to dissolve into a nightmare under heavy rain or snow. He may have to park at the guesthouse and walk the rest of the way.

The cottage is an old, run down croft of small windows, a red door of alarming brightness – Gregory suspects this is one of the renovations – and an old water trough now void of both water and farm animals. The walls have recently been whitewashed, and the odd grey scattered tile across the roof looks newer than its older brothers. Gregory drives the car around in front of the little croft and turns off the engine, John already clambering out of the vehicle.

He is pointing at a little stone outbuilding behind the cottage, in the corner of an area that might have been a garden had anyone taken any care of it. It looks as though an area of grass around the cottage has been cut, but that is far as the horticulture has gone. "Bathroom facilities," John says vaguely, before opening the front door – handle but no lock. There are two rooms inside, the doorway opening immediately onto a large kitchen. There are no modern conveniences here; to the right at the end wall there is a massive, old fashioned kitchen range with warped dark wood mantelpiece. The floor is a simple layout of large flagstones, the walls whitewashed and the ceiling is missing to reveal the roof rafters arching overhead. Facilities are basic. John has brought a cold water supply to the property, and there is a solitary tap over a Belfast sink set in a rescued wooden kitchen bench by the window. In the middle of the room there is a sturdy wooden table, engrained with scratches, cuts and decades of use, and three wooden chairs.

"Water's here." John states the obvious, turning on the tap to prove that it works. "Pure Shetland water, that. And the tour de force, the electricity." He steps proudly up to a two plug socket in the wall. "I've slowly been doing this place up over the years, but your arrival spurred me on, and I got the electric sorted. There's a light in the ceiling of each room as well. The conveniences are in the out building round the back, and there's only cold water I'm afraid. Although you don't look like a central heating softie to me..."

Gregory takes this as a compliment, although he enjoys the modern age as much as the next man, and is thinking already how much he is going to miss hot showers. Such a thing would be a weakness in John Jameson's eyes, he suspects, so he says nothing.

"... if you get desperate, you can always come up to the farmhouse to borrow the shower..."

He thinks he would rather dangle off the cliffs in bad weather and let the waves batter him clean, than go back to that unwelcoming house.

"And through here we have the second room."

Ducking his head for the low doorway, he follows John into the second and last room. This must be the bedroom for the converted cottage. Again it has the whitewashed walls, bare beam roof showing and stone flags on the floor that will be damned cold in the middle of the night. There is a fragile rocking chair in the corner of the room that he will probably avoid testing; an empty fireplace; thin cotton curtains at the windows, and a sun-bleached print of a coastline view, probably the Shetlands, in a cheap wooden frame – John's one feeble nod to the notion of interior decorating. The most imposing feature of the room is what can best be described as a giant rabbit hutch – an imposing wooden construction in the room, standing between them like a great white elephant. It is a large box on legs, with what looks like sliding doors in the front, heart-shaped holes for fingers to slip through and pull them apart.

"What is that?"

"This is a box bed." John says, a glimmer of a smile on his face as if remembering good times. "All the crofters used to sleep in these, three or four at a time, so you'll be sleeping in some luxury, having it all to yourself." He slips rough, calloused fingers into the holes and slides the doors back. "Nice and cosy in there."

Gregory stares at the legs, keeping the bed a good fifteen inches off the ground, and wonders if it's to keep him separate from the mice.

"You got a sleeping bag you can use in there?"

"I've brought all my camping gear with me," he responds. He had assumed a proper mattress for his base, somewhere to sleep out all of the roughing-it-cricks. He will have to buy a better underlay for his sleeping bag, if this oddity is to become home.

"So you'll have a wee stove for cooking with you?"

Gregory nods.

"Grand. And you'll know about the guesthouse at Lunna?"

"Yes. What do you want to do about the rent?"

"Oh, Eilidh deals with the money," John tells him. "You can see her about it. She's away the now, one of the Andersson women is giving birth. But she should be back tomorrow."

"I'll nip round soon and see her."

"Aye." John stands awkwardly in the middle of the room. "Is there anything else you'll be wanting to know?"

Gregory shakes his head, realising he's got himself into this corner, and he will have to take the cottage. Perhaps it will be an adventure, certainly an experience.

"I'll be away then," John says, leaving the room. "I'll bring round some firewood in the next few days; leave it in the lean-to at the end of the house."

The door bangs shut and Gregory is alone in his new home. He returns to the kitchen and stands at the sink, watching John Jameson striding off into one of his fields, the sheep bleating, the wind whipping across his solid, defiant figure. Gregory stuffs his hands in his jacket pockets. What the hell has he gotten himself into? His fingers touch something soft and thin, and he pulls out the red-brown feather he found by the loch, already a week ago. He holds it up to the light, examining the pattern, before setting the feather on the window sill. His first addition to the cottage. Now he has officially moved in.

The box bed quickly proves to be a hit, long before Gregory thinks he might become accustomed to it. There is something regressive, pulling him back into his childhood, about sleeping in this giant rabbit hutch. A den where he can close the doors and hide away from the world. For now he has the underlay and sleeping bag from his camping gear, a rolled up towel as a pillow – he will go into town tomorrow and get something more substantial. The interior of the box is around just six foot, for if he stretches out, head and feet almost touch the walls. At one end there is a shelf, which has already been colonised, gathering a collection of paperbacks, torch, wallet, car keys and emergency rations should he get hungry in the night. If John Jameson put his mind to it and got this place renovated – it would need a proper built in bathroom to cater for regular tourists – then the box bed could make quite a selling point for renting this out as self catering property.

The rustic basic style would prove too much for most at the moment. This means Gregory can enjoy a ridiculously cheap rent, his own space on Shetland for the next year, and probably the oddest place he will ever sleep in.

It is nearing midnight and Gregory is dozing off. He is already in the sleeping bag, the torch angled on the shelf above to shine down on his book like a bedside table. He had thought earlier that he ought to buy a cheap lamp tomorrow. If he disconnected the plug temporarily, he could feed the cable through one of the air holes, then have the lamp inside the bed. His eyes glance over the page for what must have been the fifth time. He is still not sure what this page is about; he is too tired for reading. Folding over the top corner of the page, he reaches up above his head and shelves the book, switching off the torch at the same time. He rolls onto his side and closes his eyes.

He is not sure what the time is when he wakes, although it is pitch black in the box – perhaps it is light outside although it feels too early in twilight for it to be morning. A noise has woken him, perhaps the wind outside blowing something other, creating the clatter. Nothing to worry about. At least he assumes so until there is a distinct creaking noise, like a door being opened, or the rocking chair in the corner being sat upon. Gregory opens his eyes, even though there is nothing to see in the box. This is a very old house, he reminds himself, not even a ceiling, just straight up into the roof and rafters. There are naturally going to be creaks and groans, especially out in the Shetland weather. But human instinct is irrepressible, and he feels himself grown tense.

The sound of footsteps pad through the room. Gregory is horrified, both by the sound and by his own reaction. His hands have folded into fists clutching at the edge of the sleeping bag; the sound of his racing heartbeat is thumping in his ears. This can't be explained by the weather or the age of the building. There is definitely someone or something out there, beyond the walls of his box bed, slowly walking through the room. There is a pause then a change in pace, the footsteps coming closer, and he has the distinct sensation that this thing is just on the other side of his bed wall.

He is ashamed of how afraid he is. This is hardly manly behaviour, even if there are no other witnesses. What does he think is on the other side of the wall – a monster, a trow? Or perhaps the half-rotten corpse of Andrew's dead little sister, hunting for souls to drag to limbo to play? Nothing is ever as frightening in real life as your imagination would have you believe, he scolds himself. Be a man, open the fucking door and meet this intruder, this potential thief, head on. Face your fear.

Abruptly he sits up, before he can talk himself out of direct action, mid-lurch to pull the doors open, he whacks his forehead on the side of the wall, immediately cursing and groaning. There is a flurry of movement outside, a rustling of fabric and quick footsteps running from the room and through to the kitchen. A bang of the door.

"Jesus Christ," Gregory swears, the vibrations from the collision still reverberating through his brain. He roughly slides the door open and looks out onto the empty bedroom, the faintest of touches of light filtering through the thin curtains. Dawn approaches.

He is alone in the cottage, the pensive, nervous atmosphere gone. He flops back down into his improvised bedding and closes his eyes and mentally adds a damn big padlock to his shopping list for the coming day's excursion.

When he wakes up for the second time that morning, grey light is streaming through the windows. Outside it is raining, the sky blotted by a thick blanket of concrete clouds. It looks as though it has settled for the day, if not the whole week. Considering this is Scotland, he ought to be grateful that he has already had over a week of solid sunshine upon first arrival.

In daylight hours the past, half-remembered incidents of the night seem little more than bad dreams. Gregory has almost convinced himself that there never was anyone/anything else in the cottage last night until he is standing at the sink, swilling out his coffee mug. The feather he had put on the window is missing, and in its place are two or three pieces of broken egg shell. He picks one of the shards up. It is mottled brown and beige; good camouflage for a nest made of straw and reeds. Judging from the curve and the size of the dome on this egg piece, it looks to be a little egg, perhaps three centimetres or so in length. A little egg from a little bird. He carefully replaces the artefact on the window sill, increasingly baffled. And remembers his early morning resolution that he needs to buy a padlock for the front door. Perhaps a bolt to screw on the inside wouldn't go amiss either.

He drives down the backbone of the island to Lerwick in the continuous rain. Colours are more intense, but the landscape no longer looks inviting. Today it is distinctly northern and maritime.

Lerwick, the main town of Shetland, is not a big place, although it appears as a raging giant in comparison to the other settlements on the map. Regardless, it is a small market town, with a narrow pedestrianised central shopping street. The road is paved with stone slabs, now as if varnished with the rain, a single yellow line painted down each side of the road, as if anyone would attempt to drive a car up this narrow space and dare to park. He finds a DIY shop towards the edge of the shopping area, collecting his locks and bolts as well as cheap tools to fit them. From an outdoor shop he adds to his collection of camping gear, enough underlay and pillows to make the box bed a proper little feather nest of luxury; once in he may never wish to crawl out again.

He is walking back up the shopping street, in the direction of his car, when he hears his name called out. It is strange to hear this in Lerwick, and it brings a smile to his face, as if it is the first signal that he is settling here, becoming one of the locals. He stops and looks back through the drizzle. He scans the thin crowds of tourists and shoppers, hoping for a familiar face. Nothing is recognised until a hand is reached up, waving, and he realises it is Anna-Mary, the head warden at the Sumburgh Head bird station.

She pulls the collar of her jacket up against the rain, but neglects the hood this time, hurrying towards the newcomer, her low-slung shoulder bag slapping against her rear end as she jogs, trying not to appear too eager. "I thought it was you!" she exclaims breathlessly as she catches him. "I wasn't expecting to bump into you so soon again. What brings you to Lerwick?"

"Just stocking up on a few supplies."

"You've got the new cottage now?"

"It's hardly new, but... yes."

"And it's all right?"

"Yes..." he starts, not quite sure yet how to describe it, or how his relationship with the croft will pan out in the long run. "It's certainly got personality."

Anna-Mary laughs. "That usually means it's either small or just plain odd. Which is it?"

"A bit of both," he admits. "It's definitely got character of its own. I'm sleeping in a rabbit hutch."

"What?" she laughs. "Do you mean one of those old box beds the fisher families and crofters used to have?"

"I believe it's an authentic one."

"Jesus, you are roughing it. Although not authentically. They used to get three or four people to a box. If you were married, you could have the in laws in there with you."

"What an awful thought."

"But you're not married, are you?"

The question is blurted out ever so casually, but he senses there is more to it than a need for historical accuracy. "No, I'm not."

Her eyes widen slightly, horrified that she has been so direct and blunt, but also pleased that it is done and the preferred answer has been returned. She and Astrid had discussed the matter after he had gone, coming to the conclusion that he couldn't be married or in any serious relationship if he was going to live up here on his own for a year. But they couldn't draw a line under the matter until they had confirmation direct from the source, for men and relationships could be strange, illogical things at times. "Well, then," she hurriedly continues, looking for a way to divert the focus of the conversation. "You'll be living in relative luxury, having a box all to yourself."

"Yes, even John pointed that out. I'm sure I'll be grateful for the hutch in winter." He's not sure what more to say, for Anna-Mary is gazing up at him so expectantly, so eager, that he feels he's forgotten to mention something vitally important; something she needs or wants and is prepared to wait for.

When nothing more is said, she takes the initiative. "I'm starving," she announces. "I know a great little Italian just down from here. You've got to take advantage of these things, because outside of Lerwick there aren't many eateries. You fancy grabbing a bit of lunch?"

It takes him by surprise and he has answered before he's aware of considering a response. "Yes, why not?"

The Italian restaurant has a lunch deal on pizzas, so they quickly settle for that, selecting from the menu. Anna-Mary is distracted for one so hungry, and is keen for the waiter to leave so that she can start talking again. "I was in at the opticians," she tells him without needing any prompting. "Blind as a bat."

"Oh, I hadn't realised," he says, a little awkwardly. She doesn't wear glasses; or at least not on the days he has seen her. Although he's certainly not peered too closely into her eyes to note whether she wears contact lenses.

"I wear contact lenses," she adds, stating the obvious. "I have really poor eyesight – although thankfully it's excellent when corrected. I suppose back in the old days I would have been considered blind. I certainly couldn't cope without; I'd have wandered off the edge of Sumburgh Head many a time by now without my contacts!"

"I suppose there's a lot of things we take for granted."

"It's not something I'd want to consider," Anna-Mary continues, babbling and quite aware that she is chattering but unable to stop herself. "Being blind must be just awful, don't you think?"

Gregory laughs, bemused by the comment. "I don't suppose anyone would want to lose their sight."

"Although what would be worse? Oh, thank you," she switches the line of speech for a moment as the waiter returns with their drinks. "I mean, if you had to choose between being blind, or deaf, and you had to choose. What would you go for?"

"I don't know." Gregory stares at a painting of Venice to the right of her shoulder. Either would be torture at this point. Never to be able to hear music again, to listen to birdsong, or the soothing breathing of the sea. But on the other hand to switch off colour and sunlight and movement; not to be able to see people, see their joy; watch films, gaze over a landscape. "Maybe I'd choose to be deaf."

"Everyone says that," Anna-Mary says.

"You'd rather I was blind?"

She smiles. "No. I'd choose the same. Becoming blind would reduce us to helpless children. Eyes are the windows to our souls. They are the most precious things we have."

They eat the pizzas with a more steady flow of chit chat. Anna-Mary seems to calm down when she has food inside of her. Perhaps it had just been a lack of blood sugar that had set her nerves on edge. Upon leaving the restaurant, Anna-Mary naturally falls into step with him, and they head up the road towards the car parking at the base of Fort Charlotte – a small fort atop craggy rocks, rebuilt in the 1700s; now a historic site with not much to see, and a base for the TA.

Anna-Mary spots Gregory's car parked beside a green van. "So what now?" she asks, a little disappointed that this unexpected rendez vous is to end so soon.

"I'm off to the supermarket to stock up before I head back to the cottage. There doesn't seem to be a lot in the way of shops up there."

"I see." Anna-Mary sticks her hands in her jeans pockets, standing awkwardly and mentally encouraging herself to force the words out. "Don't want company in the hutch tonight?"

He is just unlocking the door when the question comes out, and he feels himself freeze for a moment in panic. Did he really just hear that? This is the phalarope project supervisor coming on to him. Certainly for a casual moment up at Sumburgh, he'd wondered one evening what she'd be like naked and in bed, but the thought hadn't held any particular interest or realistic opportunity as things stood. He'd disregarded it, regrettably forgetting completely about her by the time he reached Fair Isle, to be distracted by the cook at the bird station. And now he was being propositioned. In his head he can hear the seconds ticking by, the longer he leaves this, the worse it will be. He catches a glimpse of her in the side mirror. She is stood behind him, blushing, already regretting that she has put herself out on such a limb. He has to say something to let her save face, to let her down gently, to allow the professional relationship to continue. It really is too early in the day to know whether he'd want anything more of her. "I've got quite a bit on in the next few days," he finally manages, a particularly feeble response that does neither of them any favours.

"Of course, you're not here on a jolly." Anna-Mary is already physically backing away from his car.

"I need to get a bit of writing done; I collected quite a bit of material on Fair Isle." And I need to get the locks fitted to the front door, he adds silently. "But..."

"Quite right," Anna-Mary interrupts quickly, not wanting to hear what follows 'but' this time. "Let me know when you're heading up to Fetlar; keep me up to date. I've got to head off myself as well. I've left Astrid on her own far too long."

Gregory straightens and watches her walk away, stony backed, shaking fingers clutching to the strap of her shoulder bag for support. Perhaps he should have said yes, but he knows that to dive into something so quickly with someone who technically is his boss would have a lot of future implications. And to be fair there has been no noticeable chemistry between them. He does not have Andrew Jameson's charm and eloquence in dealing with these kinds of scenarios. He simply does not have a high success rate with women, only having had three proper relationships. And perhaps this is why, because he does not take the few opportunities when they show up.

Back at the cottage, nothing appears to have been moved, touched or taken. He fits the padlock so that he is able to lock up from the outside, and then, as it is only lightly drizzling, he decides to take a walk by his patch of coastline. Hoping to come across a sea otter – for Shetland has a reputation for them, but the rain is thrashing down by the time he reaches a rocky cove, and it's enough to try and watch where he will put one foot in front of the other. He turns back to land, the wind lashing and trying to battle him out to sea. Wiping rainwater from his eyes, he looks to the low hills he will have to cross over to get back to the cottage. At the top there is a smallish figure, crouching in the heather, long hair or a scarf or shawl loose and flapping off to the right; rippling in the winds.

One of the neighbours, perhaps? Gregory wonders. Normally he wouldn't respond to another passing in the countryside, but as this is to be his home and the Jamesons are so uncommunicative, he will need to make as many friends here as possible. He raises an arm to wave to the figure and shouts hello although he is unsure as to whether the wind will carry his words that far. The figure makes no signal in response, motionless for a moment or two before turning and going over the brow of the hill and out of sight.

To the beat of raindrops drumming against the canvas shelter of his waterproof hood, Gregory strides through the heather, making his own pathway to the top of the hill. From his viewpoint, he scans over the saturated landscape. He is alone out here; it is as if the figure has disappeared into the rain itself.

It takes a long time to go to sleep. Although he has fitted the interior bolts, and locked himself into the cottage for the night, Gregory cannot relax, and stays awake long past the point his body wants to sleep. Part of him wishes to hear the footsteps again – to prove to himself that it wasn't his imagination. He wants to face whoever it was directly in the eye. On the other hand, it is not something he wants to get involved in, and perhaps ignorance is, as they say, bliss.

He works on his laptop at the kitchen table for some time, sifting through his notes on Fair Isle – a couple of suggested easy walks for the guidebook, a few points of interest. He listens to the rain patter against the single-pane windows, then remembers that he has yet to go up to the farm to arrange the rent with Eilidh. A pleasure to look forward to tomorrow. He then sits in the entrance to his box bed, paperback open in one hand unread, waiting for ghosts that never come.

Gregory sleeps late the following morning; surely a sign that the extra bedding purchased in Lerwick has resolved some problems. He wakes to blazing sunlight, for he did not close the box bed doors last night. There have been no visitors, the broken egg shells are still on the kitchen window sill, and nothing has been taken or added.

He plugs in the cheap kettle to one of the two sockets rigged up to the cottage, and makes a cup of strong coffee. He sits in the doorstep of the cottage, taking in the sudden change in weather. There's no fridge and cooking will be limited to the little camp stove he has brought with him unless he can be bothered to fathom to the old range, so the grocery shop has had to work around these limitations. It has created a diet of extremes – from the excessively unhealthy junk food right through to a pure raw diet of fruit and veg. He has never been particularly interested in cookery; food is something to provide the energy to keep him going, so he does not see any major disadvantage from the set up.

Taking advantage of the good weather, he walks over to the farm. Not sure how Eilidh will want to be paid, he already has enough cash for the first month in his back pocket, although he would prefer to pay by cheque or standing order. This will make life easier longer term.

The farm is quiet when he arrives. John Jameson will have already been up for hours, and will have probably already done a normal person's worth of work by now. There is the distant bleating of sheep, a light breeze, but beyond that no other sound. No cars, no rush, no pollution, no modern life. He knocks on the front door, which swings inwards a little having not been left properly on the latch. No one answers. Gregory loiters a moment then knocks again. He doesn't want to have to come back – he hasn't spoken to Eilidh about the cottage since that first dinner when she announced it was out of the question. He assumes John will have updated her on the arrangements, but he doesn't know how she will feel about this, and doesn't want to either.

Pushing the door further into the house, he leans in. "Hello? Mrs Jameson?" There is no reply, but there is a definite sound of movement from within the house. He hovers, uncertain about entering the Jameson household uninvited. But he reminds himself that he wants this matter settling now. He is here to pay them, hardly an unwelcome visitor. He goes to the kitchen, which is empty, yet he can still hear the movement, scratching and then something dropping into water. "Hello?"

No reply. He squints, concentrating on the sound. It seems to be coming from the doorway at the back of the kitchen. It leads through to the conservatory, an odd extension that can only be entered from the kitchen, set up a little like Eilidh's private retreat from the rest of the household. Stepping around the large kitchen table, Gregory heads for the back of the room, pushing the door open fully and entering the conservatory.

It is a distinctly large room. Today it is warm and bright from the sunlight. The curtains are pulled up to show off the great view that surrounds this corner of the farmhouse, comfortable chairs set around the edges, a large glass topped coffee table in the centre of the room. A few pot plants are dotted around the windowsills. The overall ambience is in stark contrast to the general disdain he first experienced at the farmstead. At the back of the room a young woman sits. She has three bowls; one to her right is filled with potatoes. She takes one potato at a time, carefully peeling it, letting the discard drop into the bowl on her lap. She then drops the clean white potato into a large bowl of water set on a small side table to her left. She has long red hair, almost waist length, and her eyes are downcast as she concentrates on her task. She wears a long-sleeved blue dress and scruffy trainers that are incongruous with the otherwise feminine look. She is back lit by the sunlight outside, catching glimmers of gold in her hair.

"Hello there," Gregory starts. "Sorry for bursting in. I was looking for Mrs Jameson."

The woman pointedly ignores him and continues to peel potatoes.

"I, er..." he falters, wondering if this is a language issue. Or perhaps, with her body hunched forward and her hair loose, the fact that she is plugged into some MP3 music device is hidden from him. He has many students in lectures these days who think he doesn't notice when they slip the little headphones into the curve of their ears. Aside from the fact that it is rude, he can never understand why they bother making an appearance at the lecture if they can't be bothered to listen.

He steps forward, leaning to the side in a comical angle, waving and hoping the movement will catch her attention. He waits for the moment that she will realise she is not alone in the room. She will pull one of the headphones from her ears and look up at him, smiling bashfully and apologising for not having heard the door. But she does none of these things, instead continuing to peel potatoes.

Eilidh hears Gregory's voice as she re-enters the house, and hurries through to the kitchen, praying he has not gone into the conservatory. But he is already there, talking and waving, trying to catch her attention. She stops in the doorway, a stone fist curling around her heart, and she watches helplessly for a moment, wishing she had returned to the house just a couple of minutes earlier. What's done is done, and she must try to salvage what she can.

"Mr. Hughson," she starts, irritated by how the morning has gone up until now, but taking a small pleasure in the way he starts at the sound of her voice, jumping and turning to look back at her.

"Mrs Jameson," he responds in kind, feeling guilty as if he has been caught thieving the family silver. "I heard a noise and I thought you were in the back of the house. I was just saying to..." he looks back to the woman, who is still peeling potatoes and ignoring both of them.

"There's no point saying anything to her," Eilidh says.

"Oh." He feels he is missing something. Eilidh looks ready to slap him. "Is she listening to music?"

"She's not listening to anything. She's deaf." She wipes her hands on her apron and stalks into the room, marching brusquely past Gregory and up to the seated woman. "And you'll get no reply either, because she's a mute as well." Turning to look back at Gregory, she puts a hand gently on the woman's shoulder. The woman immediately stops peeling, the hand with the peeler hovering mid air. She raises her head, and Gregory can see her face for the first time. Gregory smiles, waves awkwardly at her – for how do you say hello to someone who can neither hear nor speak?

Eilidh raises her eyes to the ceiling and lets out a sound of distinct frustration, as if Gregory is exceedingly dim-witted. "There's no point waving, for she cannot see you."

"What? She's blind?"

"That's the one."

Gregory peers more closely at the expressionless face. At the green clear eyes, the pupils so contracted that they have disappeared to nothing. This woman can neither see nor hear him, and even if she was aware of his presence in the room, she could not greet him, because she is a mute. A person trapped inside a faulty shell, with no way to communicate with the world. It is a little unnerving, as if trespassing on a privacy, to realise he can see her, but she must still have no idea that he is here. His eyes flicker back to Eilidh, still only beginning to appreciate the implications of such a combination of disabilities. "Who?"

Eilidh smiles tightly, as if this is painful. Her hand squeezes the woman's shoulder, who in turn places the peeler in the middle bowl, and sets the bowl on the chair. She then stands up and starts to walk as if to leave the room, moving confidently and with assurance. Her arms are by her sides, her fingers splayed out, as if testing and sensing the air as she goes. Gregory realises that the careful layout of chairs and tables, the uncluttered pathways from room to room are there for a reason, and this woman can navigate herself through the house with ease, despite her lack of so many perceptions.

"This is my daughter," Eilidh tells him, as the woman unknowingly approaches the stranger. "This is Ingrid."

She stops in front of Gregory, as if having sensed there is a foreign object now placed in her usual departure route. Her hands come up in front, a mere breath away from him, up at his chest as if to push him away or merely test to see if there is something really there. She never makes contact, her sightless eyes pointed in the direction somewhere off to the right. And yet it is enough, and she knows to side step to pass him by.

Eilidh's daughter Ingrid. She looks as though she is in her late twenties or early thirties. This must be the sister Anna-Mary had spoken of. He looks back to Eilidh. "But she's dead."

Eilidh raises an eyebrow as Ingrid leaves the room. "Evidently not. Now, is there something you wanted?"

"Yes," Gregory replies, unsettled. This has been a very surreal moment. His head is rushing through everything he has seen, has been told, fitting this new fact into the framework. Things are starting to take on new meanings. "It's about the rent. John said to speak to you about it."

"Oh yes," Eilidh nods. "Come through to the front room and I'll get you our bank account details. I find a standing order is as good as anything. Cuts out a lot of fuss and needs for visits, doesn't it? I suppose you'll be needing a receipt or some kind of bill for your expenses on this work?"

"That would be helpful."

"I'm sure I can sort something out," she says as she leads the way out of the conservatory, making the offer sound like an irritating and unnecessary task that she will begrudgingly perform to get Gregory out of the way. "There's always something that can be done."

Gregory sits in the heather and watches the blank surface of the oversized pond – calling it a loch has hints of delusions of grandeur. This is where Andrew said it was good for bird watching, but nothing has appeared to distract Gregory, and he is left with his thoughts. He twirls a feather between his fingers, another feather similar to the one he previously picked up here.

Once again he is debating with himself whether to stick this out, or try and track down John Jameson and explain that this arrangement isn't going to work out. But what reason could he give? The truth? Your family is just too disturbing. You do not behave as normal people would. He stayed in their home for two days and there was no mention or hint of Ingrid's existence. As if they'd locked her away in a cupboard – we don't like strangers coming and staring at our feeble-witted relations. The locals on the island who have distant memories of a sister are all convinced she died when she was ten years old. Even her own family behave as though she doesn't exist. Certainly she is severely handicapped and is limited in what she can do, but treating her like a leper, an outcast, will do the woman's well being and confidence no good. She must have some awareness, some senses. She must realise she is being shunned. What family could do that to their own child; their own sister?

He closes his eyes, as if to experience blindness for a minute. No colour, no movement, no shape. The entire visual field shut off. He hears the sea breeze whip over the hilltops, the cry of a lapwing in the distance. Yet he should not listen either, for Ingrid is deaf as well as blind. This entire world is closed. What is left? He feels the wind across his face, the warmth of the sun warming his skin, battling against the chill of the sea wind. He leans back and feels the unyielding, tough structure of the heather poke against his underarm. He sniffs the air, but can't pick out anything in particular other than a freshness and the lack of city living. He assumes Ingrid's sense of smell must be more specialised than this. But what kind of world experience is this, to say her sphere of perception extends to feeling and smelling. It's as if to be virtually locked inside his own head with only his thoughts for company. How would he communicate with people; how would they speak to him? With such a lack of stimuli over the years, what thoughts would one have to communicate? Without language, perhaps the thinking just stops. Perhaps she is little more than an automated doll, there to assist with household chores, and to put back in the cupboard with the vacuum cleaner and ironing board when strangers visit.

He opens his eyes again, surprisingly grateful as colours rush back. Abilities billions of people take for granted; never give a thought to. The sheer depth and variety of sight; the ability to hear birdsong; to describe an emotion in words.

He hears someone walking further up the bank, and assuming it is John Jameson, twists in his heather shrub throne to call over to the farmer. No time like the present to discuss the situation. He is taken aback to see that the approaching figure is that of Ingrid, in jeans and a dark waterproof jacket, walking surprisingly quickly and confidently through the heather.

"Ingrid!" he calls without thinking. Of course, she can't hear him. She continues forward as though he does not exist.

He pushes himself up from the heather, thinking he'll hurry up the bank and catch her, although for what purpose, and what he'll say when he does, he does not know. But the mere act of stumbling up onto his feet – for he seems to have taken root with the heather – slows her pace, and she stops, holding her hands out to her sides, but still looking straight ahead.

This reaction is unsettling. A void opens up, as if they are different species, perhaps even of different planets. She is so still, apparently doing, thinking nothing. Gregory is apprehensive; she looks as though building up to great action. Perhaps she will jump into the air and fly away. He starts up the bank towards her, and as he gets closer he notices that she shifts slightly in position to face him. She must realise someone is walking towards her. Is it the vibrations in the ground from his footsteps that she can read, Gregory wonders as he reaches her.

"Hello, it's Gregory," he starts, immediately shaking his head to himself in wonder at his own idiocy. She can't hear him. He fumbles, hovers, doesn't know what to do now that he's assumedly initiated contact. Should they just shake hands and leave it at that? In desperation, he pushes the feather he'd picked up earlier into her hand. She jumps back – it is a movement that's barely perceivable, slight and subtle. This wasn't what she was expecting. She examines the feather with her fingers, running the tip of her index finger up the side of the quill. She lifts it to her nose, breathes it in, pockets it, and starts walking again.

"Hey, wait!" Gregory calls after her. He can't stop interacting with her on his own terms. Those rules don't apply, and Ingrid's response has to be interpreted another way. But what does this departure mean? She must realise there was another person with her. Is this rudeness, or do manners simply not exist in a feeling/smelling world? Maybe she's also mentally handicapped; he hadn't seriously considered that when he was idly pondering on what the world must be like for Ingrid. So insular, so unable to communicate. So clearly physically damaged. Perhaps the brain damage extends from simply shutting off selected senses. She is a robot, a doll, but little else.

Ingrid stops walking, as if playing musical statues, and waits for a feeling that doesn't come. Something she would have felt up through the ground. She raises her arm, making an overhead scoop in the air as if she's about to swim away. She starts to walk again.

Clearly some basic communication is possible; she is not a mere doll. Gregory corrects himself, assuming this is her way of saying 'follow me'. He steps up to the level of heather she is walking through, and is surprised when his foot slips further down than expected. He's not standing on the plants themselves, but the bare earth below. It appears that Ingrid is following a track through the heather, maybe a sheep run, that isn't at first obvious to the eye. But once he starts following it, he realises how much easier it is to walk through the moorland.

She leads him through her family's farm land, away from the loch, past rises and dips in the earth, small bogs, and around the brow of a hill to a smaller loch, pebble edged, with lush glowing water. She sits down at a collection of loose rocks, hands neatly folded in her lap, her gaze straight ahead at nothing. She could be mistaken for a mannequin; no movement but strands of her hair rippling in the breeze.

Gregory steps up to her. He does not want to startle her. "I..." he starts, then stops. There is nothing he can do that will not be a surprise, so he simply sits down on a stone next to her.

Ingrid holds out the feather to him. Somehow she knows exactly where he is.

"Thank you." Now what? Is he just to sit quietly here with a mad woman, a woman whose family will not allow the rest of the world to see? Keeping her locked in a cupboard, out of shame, or perhaps out of consideration for strangers.

She suddenly sweeps onto him, taking his hands and terrifying him in the process. It's as if she's trying to attack, but in being blind, can't find him and instead ineffectively batters at his fingers. Maybe this is just a strange fit. Madness. Perhaps she will dig her fingernails into his flesh. He watches, utterly bemused as her fingers fly across his hands, tapping and stroking and pointing. In other circumstances it could have been erotic, but there doesn't seem to be anything seductive about this; in fact it feels urgent, frustrated. It slowly dawns on him that there is nothing random about her actions. There is a pattern, a method. She's talking to him. He has no idea what she is saying.

Abruptly, she stops, sits up and holds her hands out as if waiting for a reply. What can he do? He has no way to tell, or sign to her that he doesn't understand. With no other idea to mind, he places the palm of his hand flat down on hers and hopes he isn't saying something he'll later regret.

She looks pensive, as if waiting for something to start. There is nothing. She pushes his hand away, then starts again on his fingers, only this time much more slowly. She then waits for a response, but he has nothing to offer. Realising this is to be a one sided conversation, she stops trying.

"I'm sorry, I can't..."

Her arm flies out as if to silence him. Pointing to the loch.

There is something dabbling, paddling in the edge of the water closest to them. A small bird with a long, pointed dark beak and plumage a mixture of chestnuts, browns and reds. Gregory takes his binoculars out of his jacket pocket and focuses in on the bird. It is a red-necked phalarope.

He feels a wide grin spreading across his face. Andrew hadn't been wrong. Even if he had no idea where the birds were. And in offering up a feather, she has understood and led him straight to the feeding ground. He hadn't even realised this little loch was on the Jameson property.

Lowering his binoculars, he turns to thank Ingrid, or at least attempt to thank her, but she is no longer there. Already up and away walking through the heather – a solitary figure retreating into the background.

When Gregory returns to the crofter's cottage for a late lunch there is a plastic bag of what looks like papers hanging from the padlock. One of the corners of the bag has ripped, leaving a streamer of white plastic to ripple out in the breeze; a low sound like a cheap flag of rubbish. Unwinding the plastic handles from his do-it-yourself security, he unlocks the door and steps into the kitchen. John Jameson must have been by – Gregory wonders for a moment if the farmer will be irritated the padlock signifies a lack of trust for the local area – but it is only a moment and in truth Gregory doesn't care. He doesn't want another night of locals sneaking about trying to scare the city boy.

Dropping the papers onto the table, he fills the kettle with ice cold water and sets it onto its base on the floor, flicking it on to boil water. Whilst the water is warming up, he sits at the table and looks at the bag. Is this a contract – John Jameson doesn't strike him as the kind of man who has a great need for bureaucracy. Shaking out the bag, he lets the contents slip onto the rough table top. Thin pamphlets and booklets, that actually look like school textbooks from the eighties. Is this a mistake? Wrong door? Although there are so few doors in the area, it is difficult to believe this could have been left at the wrong place. Taking up the first book, he flicks distractedly through it, surprised to find that there are very few words in it; in fact it is mostly black and white line drawings of hands. As he flicks through at speed, the hands move position, as if they are waving at him. He shuts the booklet and looks at the front over again. There is a narrow strip of plastic tape stuck across the top, not at a neat balanced level with the top of the book. It looks quite battered, with lumps and bends in the otherwise smooth tape.

Returning to the first page of the book, the introduction, he realises this is a beginner's guide to British sign language. In this volume you will learn the alphabet and the number system. The first few pages explain how to sign the numbers one to ten, which is easy as it's simply a case of holding the relevant number of fingers up. In a perverse moment, Gregory wonders how the maimed deaf cope in this situation. Are the numbers nine and ten a no go? From there the book patiently explains the alphabet so that learners will quickly be able to communicate through the painstaking method of finger spelling. Gregory glances through the letters, surprised to find a few familiar signs from what Ingrid had tapped onto his fingers like Morse code that morning. She must have realised that he couldn't understand, but furthermore that there is something she wants to say even now that she knows he can't understand. Because she is now saying – in her own way – that he is to learn her language.

He puts the book down and takes a quick look through the other volumes. There are more advanced sign language, moving from finger spelling to the actions and signs for whole words, aiming for a fluency he's only ever seen on the odd occasion on the television when the sign language translator appears in the bottom corner of the screen, a miniature like a pixie of the media world. Although not of much use for someone who cannot see.

There is another book of basic alphabet which he almost disregards as a duplicate before realising that this is an alphabet for two people, rather than one. This is the alphabet of the deaf blind. A way to speak in sign language to someone who cannot see. It is quite similar to the standard sign language alphabet, only that the signs are made into the blind person's palm or hand. It invites an intimacy that usually does not come from casual chit chat.

There is a click and a plume of steam from the floor as the kettle comes to the boil. Gregory looks over to his laptop and knows that he ought to do some work – either that or go out exploring new material for the book. But the new and quite unexpected project before him is far more tempting. Doesn't everyone want to learn a new language? OK, he negotiates with his good sense. I will read up on the alphabet today, and call the student working up on Fetlar and arrange a time to go up for a few days' of bird watching. That way he can feel productive, but also feed his curiosity for this new communication. Besides which, he gets the distinct impression Ingrid Jameson doesn't get many people to talk to, and possibly has years worth of conversations lined up waiting for someone to listen. Out of charitable consideration for his fellow man, he ought to learn the basics. He picks up the first book on the alphabet and wonders for a moment if he is about to open up a whole new can of worms.

He wakes with the dawn the next morning, pushing open the box-bed door, to lie lazily and gaze absently at the window. It is so utterly silent here, at least void of the noise of human development – no cars, no electricity, no general clatter and excitement as the world goes about its business. Just the sound of the sea, of the wind, and the birds; the occasional rumblings and bleatings of the sheep in distant fields.

Drinking instant coffee, he sits and flicks back through the deaf alphabet. It's quite logical and not too difficult to remember. He spells out coffee, a C made in the curve of the thumb around to first finger; O being the fourth vowel, pointed out on the third finger after thumb; F is two fingers together tapped across the knuckles of two fingers together on the left hand; E is the second vowel and so is pointed out on the first finger after the thumb. That would be if she could see. What of the deafblind alphabet? He opens the leaflet and studies the adaptations to create the letters in another person's hand.

The morning is fresh, the grass still damp with dew as he leaves the cottage, marching out up to the hill to skirt around the stone-walled sheep fields and back towards the moorland, the small lochs and the feeding grounds of the red necked phalarope. He wants to see the little bird again; to be sure it wasn't just a fluke; that it really does take up residence here on the Jameson farm.

He is soon back at his viewing station by the collection of rocks, pleased when the bird soon puts in an appearance, dabbling at the edge of the water, paddling around in circles, picking up food from the surface of the water. It looks like such a dainty, fragile creature, that might just blow away in the wind, but the phalarope is a resilient bird, despite its painfully low numbers in the UK, and would be quite as happy feeding on open water, as it was now in this sheltered spot.

A loose rock is upended and clatters over the rock pile. Although he is wide awake and reacts immediately to the sound, Gregory doesn't jump or panic at the noise. He doesn't know what it is, but casually lowers his binoculars and looks across. Ingrid Jameson is approaching. How the hell could she know that he was sat here watching the birds? Or maybe she hasn't realised that he is here, and was out on a stroll and decided to have a sit at her favourite stopping off place on her well-worn route around the farm property.

"Morning," he says, out of habit, because he cannot help himself. Talking for no good reason, he, a man who has been accused by past girlfriends of not talking enough, of being too much of a silent type.

Ingrid ignores him, as is her way. She carefully picks a route across the rocks to the boulders big enough for sitting. She seems more cautious today, as if knocking over a rock has unbalanced the landscape as she sees it in her mind. She has no idea what might have changed. As she steps up to him, she puts a hand on his shoulder, not startled that it is there, and swings herself around to sit down on the boulder next to him. She draws her knees up, hunkers forward, her hands set on her lap, and stares out at nothing.

Gregory puts down his binoculars. He is both keen and nervous to try out this new alphabet, to see how much he really can remember now that he does not have the charts in front of him at the kitchen table. But how to initiate conversation? Her hands replace her eyes, her ears and her mouth; they multitask, and they are quite different tools to the hands most of the human race possess. It feels like an invasion of her personal space to take her left hand; for taking and clutching onto hands hold entirely different connotations in the sphere Gregory has come from. Even now, gingerly taking her pale hand, he feels something, a spark or some electricity, that is entirely one-sided, and he feels distinctly awkward. On taking her hand, he would expect her to respond, to turn slightly to look at him, as if to signal, 'yes, I'm listening'. But from Ingrid there is nothing. No movement, no facial expression. She continues to stare at the loch without seeing it, as if he isn't there with her.

Might as well just go for it, Gregory thinks, considering she hasn't slapped him or pulled away. He spells out his first sentence to her that she can hear, slowly, haltingly, a space between each letter. There is no fluency, no speed, and he slowly says the words out loud to himself to keep track of where he is. Whilst the alphabet is relatively simple, logical; he hasn't considered how difficult this might be. Any language takes a lot of practice to reach the point where communication works with speed, fluency, a comfort that one does not need to actively think about what one is doing.

I: Third vowel. Gregory touches the tip of Ingrid's middle finger.

A: First vowel. He touches the tip of her thumb.

M: His three fingers set rigid together, placed out in the palm of her hand. He is surprised by how cool her hand is. She is used to this of course; he on the other hand feels as though he is taking liberties with a young woman he barely knows.

G: He balls his hand into a fist and places it in the palm of her hand.

R: He curls his first finger, the shape of a backwards r, and again places it in the palm of her hand. So much of this is marking out communication into the palm of her hand, the lines of her future and life marked out on soft skin. He wishes his name was shorter, whilst conversely wishing it was much longer.

E: Second vowel: Fingertip to fingertip of first fingers.

G: Another fist into the palm.

O: Fourth vowel: Fingertip to second-to-last finger.

R: A curled finger in the palm.

Y: He points to the base of the curve going down the inside of her thumb and up against her first finger.

Introductions complete. Almost. He uncertainly holds onto her hand for a moment longer, before letting go. She is still staring at the lake. Nothing. Surely he hadn't misunderstood the alphabet that much had he? Or the reasons for those books – she is the only person who could have plausibly left them there. Because she wants to communicate.

Nothing, and then, barely noticeable at first, there is movement at the corner of her lips, before she breaks out into a smile. So strange, because it is a facial expression she can't see; she can't have learned if from other people. Perhaps these shows of emotions on the face are deeper, instinctual. Gregory can't help grinning back. It is beautiful.

She shuffles around on her rock, and holds up her hands, spelling out a word in the standard deaf alphabet – for she knows he is watching, that he can see, and there is no need to take his hands.

"*Ingrid.*" She has understood him, and is replying. And whereas Gregory stutters and stumbles over saying his name, her fingers move gracefully, fluidly. It is a leap from awkwardly written separate letters, written by a pencil in a fist, to flowing, stylish handwriting. Like calligraphy.

She starts on something else, jumping in complexity straight away to a full sentence, but it is too quick, and after a few letters he is lost again. This is certainly not going to be as easy as he first assumed. He catches her wrist, and she starts again, this time more slowly, as if talking to a child.

"*You were at my mother's house?*"

He nods. "Yes." Then shakes his head. He must remember that she can't see or hear; nodding or speaking won't help. "*Y-E-S.*"

She smiles, amused by some private joke, then abruptly reaches across and grabs his hand. He is not as pliable as she is used to being, and it takes a little awkwardness, as if she is trying to break his fingers, to get the position she wants. Taking his first finger, she taps it twice into the palm of his hand, then spells out the word YES for him. She then takes his finger again and rubs it gently back and forth across her palm as if trying to warm up. Oh Jesus, Gregory thinks, in other circumstances this could be getting erotic. There was something about the slightest of touches...

Ingrid is already off, dropping his hand to spell out the word NO. Shortcuts for communication.

He takes her hand, which is trusting, loose, ready to be formed, touched. "*P-E-A-L-I-N-G-P-O-T-A-T-O-E-S.*"

Ingrid's face is animated, her body language, her movements so alive in comparison to that day he first saw her, a living doll with no thought or emotion; robotically peeling potatoes, moving through the room to leave when Eilidh had joined them. "*I know,*" she signs. "*That was the day we first met properly.*"

"Properly met?" Gregory asks no one. Besides which, how could she have known it was him. Or that he was the same person as yesterday, or the person who is staying in the old cottage. How can she know that anyone is staying in the old cottage? He thinks back to that first night in his new home, awake in the box bed, convinced that someone or something was creeping through the cottage.

"*You were in my mother's house a week ago.*"

"*Yes.*"

"*Why?*"

"*I A-M R-E-N-T-I-N-G T-H-E C-O-T-T-A-G-E.*"

Ingrid has already guessed this much. "*Why?*"

"*I A-M W-R-I-T-I-N-G A G-U-I-D-E-B-O-O-K A-B-O-U-T S-H-E-T-L-A-N-D.*"

"*How did you contact my mother about the cottage?*"

"*I L-I-V-E I-N E-D-I-N-B-U-R-G-H. I K-N-O-W A-N-D-R-E-W.*"

Ingrid looks a little irritated by this piece of information. Perhaps she hadn't realised that Andrew had come home for a visit. He hadn't spent that much time in the family home, it is possible that he did not possible to go say hello to his disabled sister. Gregory wonders where Ingrid lives; for he had not seen any sign of her presence in the farm house.

"*How long will you be here?*"

"*A Y-E-A-R.*"

"*Are you a student?*"

"*No. I T-E-A-C-H A-T T-H-E U-N-I-V-E-R-S-I-T-Y.*"

She seems a little surprised by this, and takes his hand again, but not for signing. She runs her fingers over the surface, examining knuckles, calluses, the leathery, weather-worn male skin, as if checking over assumptions she has previously made. *"How old are you?"*

Gregory laughs out loud. Clearly older than you first assumed, he thinks. He wonders if his hands do betray his real age, or if they are misleading. He counts out the numbers on her fingers. A three and a six. Thirty-six.

"I am thirty-one."

This surprises Gregory, although really it should be expected. Andrew is thirty-four going on fourteen, and Ingrid is the younger sister that the locals seem to assume died. Of course she would be somewhere around the turn of thirty. Ages can be hard to judge from mere appearances. There is something youthful, uncorrupted about her. Almost ageless.

"What is your subject?"

"My subject?" Gregory wonders, caught unawares by the sudden change again in conversation.

Ingrid rewords her question already. *"What do you teach at university?"*

"G-E-O-G-R-A-P-H-Y."

"I've not studied geography very much."

This comment surprises him. Another preconceived idea. That someone so lacking in the means to communicate, the access to language barred, wouldn't take part in education to any major level.

"Y-O-U S-T-U-D-Y?"

"Mostly literature and history," she signs. *"I take Open University Courses for fun."* She looks disgruntled, as if not convinced by what she is telling him. She leans back against the rocks. *"What else is there for me to do here?"*

Live music, the production of a solo artist, flows out of an open window. Gregory walks down the short drive towards the rear of Lunna Guesthouse. He passes a red letterbox embedded in a chunk of stone wall bisecting the field wall that lines the narrow track – a symbol of communication with the outside world. He has his hands in his jacket pockets, collar pulled up against the wind that has steadily picked up over the afternoon.

One of the locals has brought their fiddle to the guesthouse for the evening; Gregory has noticed that this tends to happen a lot, on the spur of the moment, simply because they can and they are in the mood for a little music. As he walks into the bar, he sees the musician is the salmon farmer, Calum Moran, who had been at the bar the previous time Gregory was here with Andrew. That already feels like another era, Andrew dissolving from the locality as easily as he had arrived, as if he had never existed to begin with.

Calum leans back in the window seat to see who has just entered. He nods a hello to Gregory, his fingers dancing across the violin strings without a thought. Gregory still wonders at the degree of musical talent on these islands; people practised to the extent that music is an unconscious thought, rather like the beating of a heart. That it is as instinctual as breathing.

"Gregory, you've joined us," Miriam Rea, the landlady of the Lunna Guesthouse, greets him. She is a skinny woman, barely enough to stand up to the Shetland winds; brown hair twisted with salted grey. At first glance not much to look at, but she has a spritely way about her that makes her seem a lot younger than her forty something years. Gregory is a little bemused by the surprise in her voice, as it had been Miriam who had stopped by the cottage that afternoon to tell him they were serving food tonight. They'd had a good deal on a glut of scallops and needed all hands to the deck to get the food they would be preparing eaten. Gregory is bored of cans of soup or baked beans, and is glad of not having to put any effort into preparing food this evening.

He slides onto a bar stool. "Did you get many takers?"

Miriam's eyes are bright. "Oh yes, I think pretty much everyone I caught up with is coming. We'll have a right knees up tonight."

"Are the Jamesons coming?"

The easy flow of music breaks as Calum starts laughing.

Miriam raises her eyebrows. "You can tell you've not been here long."

"What's up with Calum?" Jayne Castleton, wife of one of the local sheep farmers, pauses in the doorway and looks from Calum, to Gregory and Miriam.

"Gregory had just asked if the Jamesons were coming."

"The Jamesons?" Jayne coughs. "I thought we explained last time you were here that they keep themselves to themselves. Andrew's the only one who really comes in."

"Aye, and that's only once a decade," Miriam adds.

"You can't blame the man for leaving that God-forsaken place," Calum says, setting his violin down. He strides over to the bar to fetch his pint that he has neglected up until now. "They're not into socialising. It must be fair lonely up there, just John and Eilidh. That wee brat, Shea, isn't there that often."

Gregory is perplexed. "Just John and Eilidh?"

Jayne, a young woman only in her early thirties, but already with a ruddy touch to her cheeks and a swelling mid section that may just be unshed pregnancy weight, or the beginnings of child number three – no one knows but there is much discussion in the bar when she is not in the building – gives Gregory a curious look. "You'll know better than the rest of us. You stayed in that house a couple of nights."

"Paying tenant now," Calum adds.

"Yes, you'll be more of a permanent feature than the children, what with Andrew living on the mainland and Shea tarting her way through Lerwick," Miriam says.

"If you don't count the ghost," Calum jokes.

Jayne scowls at him. "Don't you start on Hugo."

Gregory is losing the thread, a flurry of names and local references. Things he has not grown up with. "Hugo is a ghost?"

This sets Calum off, choking on his beer.

Miriam leans over the bar, patting Calum's hand. "No," she tells Gregory. "Hugo is Jayne's husband; he'll be joining us shortly. And he's very much alive, certainly the last that I saw him. He's just convinced there is a ghost living on the Jameson farm."

"The ghost of Ingrid Jameson." Jayne raises her orange juice as if to suggest a toast.

"Ingrid's not a ghost," Gregory scoffs.

"This is what I say," Jayne continues. "No such thing. But Hugo reckons he sees her roaming the moors now and then..."

"Now and then after a drink," Calum mutters.

Jayne pointedly ignores the comment. "I don't know what he sees, but I'm sure it's not Ingrid Jameson. She died years ago. Maybe John's got a fancy woman who comes sneaking onto the farm. God only knows he'd need one, living with the likes of Eilidh."

Gregory feels uncomfortable. It is true what they say; a little knowledge is a dangerous thing. He feels that he has not been properly briefed on what he should say, what he can disclose. Suddenly Ingrid feels like a great secret. She's no ghost. She exists. But in such a close knit community, where everyone has an eye on one another's business, how can they not know that Ingrid exists? If Ingrid is even more isolated from the world than her parents are, whose choice has this been?

After Miriam had been by the cottage to let him know they'd be serving food that evening, he had wondered about trying to track Ingrid down and see if she wanted to come. In the last few days since they have first met, he has seen her every day. He has fallen into the habit of taking a walk around the farm every morning, and at some point she silently appears, somehow sensing where he is. This morning he had told her about his project work on the phalarope and his trip to Fetlar to see the main recorded site for the birds. He will be travelling up there tomorrow. She seemed a little irritated by this news; perhaps by the fact that no sooner has she found a source of conversation, then it is to depart again. He had wondered about seeing if she wanted to come down to Lunna House for a change. He doesn't suppose she has the most exciting of evenings at home. But then he thought that she might feel isolated, as people chat, grow merry on drink and listen to music, whilst she is excluded, unable to see or hear. That and people might get the wrong idea. But now he sees that it was probably for the best. If everyone thinks she is dead, it would hardly do to stroll casually into the bar with her on his arm.

"But are we sure she's dead?" Miriam questions. "There was never a funeral."

"Are you sure about that?" Jayne contests. "I'm sure I have a memory of..."

"I don't know what you're remembering, but it was never Ingrid Jameson's burial. I remember they had to take her out of school because she went blind." Miriam turns to Gregory. "Turned blind overnight. Just like that, imagine it, waking up and suddenly you can't see a thing. Must have been terrifying. Of course the primary school wasn't equipped to deal with something like that. I wonder if she's living somewhere else, in a home for the disabled."

"Who knows," Calum says. "But have you seen the ghost of Ingrid Jameson?" he asks Gregory. "You're living on the farm. You're our eyes and ears there now."

Our eyes and ears. The two redundant features of Ingrid, at least the two main redundancies, for she cannot speak either. Gregory is unsure of what to say. He feels as though he is privy to a secret. He should not say anything until he has asked Ingrid about these strange arrangements. "There's no ghosts or ghouls on the farm that I've noticed," he says, not telling a lie, only avoiding the truth.

More people filter into the bar; the group relocate to the tables as the food comes out. Gregory finds he is at a corner table with a Norwegian tourist; Calum at the next table frequently leaning over with more local gossip. The Norwegian woman, Eline, seems a little bemused and amused by all of the tales. She is cycling around the Shetlands, having come over on the summer ferry from Bergen. She is exploring the localities at the slow pace of the bike, and is clearly enjoying the fact that she has fallen lucky at this place, with plenty of conversation and a welcome for strangers. She explains to Gregory that she no longer feels the need to sleep out in the open, and prefers the convenience of hot water and a comfortable bed in a guest house whenever she can. She has taken a month off work, and intends to cycle around as many of the islands as she can manage. She is interested to hear of the guidebook Gregory is working on, wishing there was something like that already available – it would have been good to have a better idea of what accommodation was available where before she had set off on this crazy adventure.

As the evening wears on, they move to the window seat with a bottle of whisky, listening to Calum on the fiddle, accompanied by Jayne Castleton on the accordion. Eline lights up with a warm glow, her clear skin beaming with health as she grows drunk. Her very blonde hair falls out of the ponytail as she laughs along with the tall tales and jokes being traded across the bar. By the time midnight has passed, Gregory thinks he can feel the earth starting to move beneath his feet. He is warm and comfortable, too happy and thoughtless to really care about anything. He lets Eline take him up to her room without any thought towards what will happen beyond the next moment. All he thinks of now is how he will put one foot in front of the other to get up the stairs.

He wakes early in the morning, silver grey light filtering through the window, the wind rattling urgently at the loose glass in the frame. He puts a hand to his head. It has been a while since he has been properly hung over. He is too old for this student-like behaviour. This is the kind of thing Andrew would do. Struggling up from the bed, he staggers across to the en suite bathroom, and for a long time drinks cold water greedily from the tap like a dog. He is going to have to drive up north, take two ferries to get to Fetlar, he thinks. He will perhaps take a later ferry, for he needs to sober up.

The digital alarm clock on the side of the bed says it is five in the morning. There is still time to sleep off the worst of this feeling. On the bed Eline is fast asleep, bed sheets twisted around her legs. She is lying stretched out on her back, utterly naked in a careless, Scandinavian way. One arm is thrown up over her head, pulling her flesh taught across her torso. She looks distinctly flat-chested.

He runs a hand over his face. What has he been doing? Gregory really isn't the type for one night stands, possibly because he so rarely gets propositioned. Padding across to the window, he pushes back the net curtain to peer outside. Eline's room looks out of the back of the house, and there is a clear view of the main road running up away from Lunna and along the edge of the land towards the Jameson farm. There is a figure walking down the main road towards Lunna with a touch of uncertainly. The figure is waving something in front, as if brushing away debris, but as Gregory stares closer, he realises it is a white stick, and it is scanning the road ahead for obstacles. He squints through the dawn light. It is Ingrid Jameson walking down the road. What is she doing away from the farm? Someone might see her – then the locals will know for definite that she is no ghost.

There is a snort as Eline coughs at something in her sleep. Gregory glances back at her as she rolls onto her front, flinging an arm out and knocking a book off the bedside table. When he looks back to the road it is empty, as if Ingrid was a ghost that simply blew away with the wind.

The knock on the car window is barely louder than the constant drum of rain. Gregory doesn't notice it for a moment, and jumps when he sits back up and discovers the figure at the window. He has just pulled up in a small – four car capacity – car park at the edge of a loch. The car park is merely a splurge of tarmac off the side of the main road; that in itself a single tracked, solitary dead end road for the entire island. This is Fetlar. A small island off the eastern side of the Shetland mainland. Fetlar is relatively flat, undulating landscape of green and rocks, with occasional villages – Shetland style with groupings of scattered houses and farms. With two local ferry rides to get here, and a main road that doesn't even manage a circuit of the island, this feels like the definition of isolated.

The figure at the driver's door is the student living on Fetlar for the summer. He looks like a boy, although Anna-Mary had assured Gregory that Ivan was a slightly older student, at the majestic old age of twenty, perfectly old enough to be left on his own. Apparently there were to be two students, for it wouldn't do to abandon one young person alone in this isolated environment, but the other student simply couldn't hack it, and fled after three days, clambering for alcohol, cigarettes and parties.

Gregory shrugs the hood of his waterproof jacket over his head and opens the door, stepping into the torrents.

"Gregory Hughson?" the young man asks, shouting above the rain.

Gregory nods.

"I'm Ivan. We spoke on the phone."

"That we did." Gregory gazes out across the loch, Loch Funzie, the usually calm surface pitted by the rain. Beyond there is a slight hill; rough grassland reigns where the water has not reached, and is typical of Shetland, not a tree in sight. It gives the sensation of everything, sky included, being low to the ground, close to the level of the sea. It doesn't look like there's any shelter anywhere. He turns to Ivan. "Do you have any kind of a hide set up?"

"Better than that, there's a proper hide." Ivan waves his arm out across the loch. "It's a short walk, just a few hundred meters. Better bring anything you want with you."

Gregory gets his rucksack out of the back of the car, and locks up. Ivan leads the way, continuing down the road from the car park, along the length of the loch. There is a brown road sign pointing to the marshy grasslands, and a footpath crossing over a style. From here, the footpath leads them away from the road and the loch, cutting through the fields and arriving at a wooden hide looking out onto what is referred to as the mires of Funzie, a marshy area with ponds and reeds as nature intended with no sign of man. Gregory's first view of this wilderness is from the viewing slit of the hide; the horizon cut up by the torrential rain.

"Jesus, I've picked a great time to come up to Fetlar," he comments as he takes off his raincoat, droplets of water shaking to the floor.

"It's bound to pick up at some point," Ivan says, sounding unconvinced.

Gregory looks over the collection Ivan has been building in the hide. There's a telescope set up at one of the viewing slits, a pair of binoculars and note pad on a shelf just ready for action. A rucksack is dropped thoughtlessly at the back of the hide, opened with food spilling out. Ivan is taking a large thermos flask out, along with two plastic cups. "Can I offer you a cup of tea?"

Gregory can't help but laugh. "All the mod cons here?"

"Something like that."

"Might as well. I don't suppose we're going to see a lot just now."

"No, the rain is too heavy. Although they're tough little birds. Bit misleading, when you think about how dainty they look. Must be a bit of a disappointment," he adds as he pours hot water into the cups, adding cheap teabags to the mix. "Come all the way to Fetlar for your first look at the phalaropes, and they're hiding out of the rain."

The steam curls up into the damp, chilled air. Gregory hopes this isn't to be base camp, but then again he can't see any sleeping bags or other signs of permanent habitation. "I've already seen them," he says. "It turns out there's a pair nesting near a wee loch close to where I'm staying."

"I didn't think you were on Fetlar."

"I'm not; I'm on the mainland, near Lunna."

"Lunna?" Ivan isn't familiar with the name. This is his first time on Shetland, and he hasn't spent a lot of time looking into the geography of the islands.

"It's a peninsula off the east coast, quite far up the main island," Gregory explains, picking up the cup to warm his hands.

"And do we know about this?"

"*We* in our professional standing?"

"Something like that."

"No. The family at the farm know, that's about it. It's an important find. I don't think it's going to knock Fetlar's standing though; this is the stronghold after all. It's more of an outpost."

"Fetlar does have ninety percent of the UK's population."

"Something like that."

"I was wanting to try and get some surveying done on the north side of the island whilst you're here, if you're up for helping with that," Ivan says. "Anna-Mary doesn't want me wandering off into the wilds too much on my own. I don't know what she thinks is going to happen."

"She is responsible for you. Did they not manage to get another student? It must be a bit dull up here on your own."

"They left it too late. Sarah walked out after three days; there wasn't really time to arrange for anyone else." Ivan shrugs. "She was annoying; I can't say I miss her. God knows why she'd signed up for this. She really wasn't the right kind of person for it. Not that it's awful here. It's not too bad. There's a little bod we've got to use in Funzie; it's a bit basic, but it's pretty snug in there. I don't mind the quiet, the lack of people."

It is a good thing that Ivan is happy in his own company, Gregory thinks later that day when he is in the bod. Funzie is not a fun place, certainly not the kind of fun the other student, Sarah, would have been hoping for. There is nothing wrong with the sparse hamlet; in fact in moments of irritation with the human population in general, this is the kind of place that looks idyllic to Gregory. He is not a city dweller naturally, but in pursuing a career in academia, he has had to compromise on this point.

Funzie is a village at the end of the road on Fetlar. Village in the general sense of the word does not capture the spirit of the place. There is no obvious centre or gathering, rather that it seems for a short distance along the main road, there are more houses than usual scattered over the green landscape. There are no shops or facilities here; the only shops on the island are further back up the road in the slightly larger village of Houbie, and even there the availability and opening hours are limited. There is no petrol station on the island – Gregory hadn't realised before he'd driven over, and quickly thinks back to the fuel gauge – he should have enough to get back to the nearest petrol station on Yell.

Despite the rain, Ivan is outside the bod having a cigarette. Gregory sits on one of the bunks inside, feeling like the father in this excursion. There isn't really a big enough age gap, if he was Ivan's father, he would have been sixteen when he was born. But driving up to Funzie from the car park, Ivan in the passenger seat, Gregory feels like the responsible adult in the collective. The father, or at the very least, the teacher. He is falling back into old roles, even though he had intended this year to be a complete break from teaching.

"Reading anything good?" Ivan appears in the doorway, the smell of nicotine hanging around him like an aura.

Gregory glances back at the open book in his hands – he has been day dreaming and staring at the same page without seeing it for the last five minutes. It is another of the books Ingrid has lent him – again it is back to school; this time with homework. This is part one of sign language proper, the hand signs for words as a whole, rather than having to spell everything out. To speed up conversation and communication. It's not something Gregory can actively use, because Ingrid cannot see; but she will use the standard deaf alphabet and words to communicate if she knows she is being watched. She wants to speed up her conversation; more than likely frustrated by having to drop down to painfully slow baby talk to speak to Gregory.

He holds up the book. "British sign language."

"Sign language?" Ivan is surprised. "Is this so we don't disturb the birds?"

Gregory smiles lightly. Why is he putting so much effort into this? In truth, he feels as though it is something he must learn. He will be here for a year, without sign language he simply can't communicate with Ingrid. And if he can't talk to her, he will be letting her down. If she is a great secret with only her parents and sister to talk to – Andrew can't count for he is so rarely on the islands. Her small social circle must make dull company after a time. Gregory doesn't want to overestimate his own role, but after all these isolated years, he must be like hidden treasure.

"There's a woman on the farm where I'm renting the cottage who is deaf-blind."

"Shit," Ivan walks into the room, taking his jacket off. "That's rough. So you're learning to talk to her." He pauses, making assumptions on the basis of the disability. She must be an old woman, an old crone. "Is she worth talking to that much?"

Gregory runs his finger down the edge of the book. He doesn't have to consider the question. "Yes," he answers. "If nothing else, she knew where the phalaropes were on the farm. She's worth knowing."

"And she's deaf *and* blind?"

"I have no idea how, but she knows. She goes out walking on her own over the farm."

"Jesus. She can't be that old then; I mean, I was imagining an old woman."

"Early thirties."

"That is rough. To be deaf or blind would be bad enough, but to not have either..." Ivan sits down. "I just can't imagine it. Not to be able to see or hear anything. How do you actually experience the world? You wouldn't have any sense of depth..." he drifts off again, going into a poetic moment as he tries to empathise. It is impossible to truly appreciate. He wonders why Gregory is learning the language – it looks as though he is putting some considerable effort in, which seems like overkill just to find out that a pair of phalaropes nest locally. But on the other hand, when you are out on the islands, with no television, internet and modern living, it is amazing how much time you grasp back. So much time for reading, reflecting, certainly the perfect conditions for learning a new skill, such as a language.

He and Ivan spend a couple of full productive days watching the birds and walking the north coast of the island, checking for more breeding pairs. He spends his final morning researching for the guide book, making a note of the public services – what there are of them – as well as some points of interest. He will be back to Fetlar at some point, but it is worthwhile gathering some information whilst he is here. There is a small museum in the centre of the island, telling of the history, the lives and the hardships, and even a few colourful local characters: strong men, storytellers, gentry building follies and observatories, and a curious tradition of the skeklars, children dressed up as what looks like haystacks, out at Halloween to visit neighbours and dance and make noise.

Gregory cuts his stay on Fetlar short by half a day when he hears from Ivan that Anna-Mary is coming up that afternoon. He cannot face her, her eagerness, that keen, hopeful tint in her eyes, like a needy dog desperate to please. After Eline he can't even claim the moral high ground of not partaking in one night stands shacking up in a box bed. It was essentially what she had been suggesting, although he suspects once started, Anna-Mary wouldn't be satisfied with one night.

Whilst parked up at the ferry 'terminal' (the main road broadens out into four lanes which abruptly drop into the sea) to travel back across to Unst, Gregory thinks he sees Anna-Mary drive off the ferry when it arrives. He is ashamed to say he looks away, not wanting her to notice him, and is glad when the arriving cars have headed onto the island and the waiting passengers are guided on the ferry. He has escaped for this time.

The rain drums on the roof like an airborne machine gun attack. It thunders against the window panes, and Gregory is half convinced the raindrops are running down the inside of the glass. It does not feel like the most securely constructed cottage, and there are draughts of many angles. He will have to get some practice for making fires before winter comes so that he can keep the cottage warm. Perhaps it was not such a clever idea to take a cheap year off work and stress, beetling through part time assignments, master of his own time, and living on a low rent. This cottage will suffer from the cold and the damp, and perhaps he will cripple himself through this sabbatical.

He stands at the window, examining the rain-distorted landscape beyond. He had intended taking a walk this morning; perhaps even a drive to a nearby locality for some exploring. Perhaps not. Today is the time for writing up notes, reading and general inactivity. Sweeping his waterproof jacket over his head like a cape, he grabs his car keys and hurries outside to fetch a few things from the car. He was too tired to unpack last night. As he turns to head back inside, he is startled to see a figure out in the rain. Ingrid is by the door, in a shapeless raincoat, the hood shadowing her face and her body shrugged back into the depths of the coat.

"Ingrid!" he calls out, hoping she hasn't been out here long, as he has not heard a tap at the door. Of course she doesn't react, doesn't hear him. As he runs across, she signs hello – she must realise by whatever means and senses she works with, that he has left the cottage and is out in the rain with her.

"You need to come in from the rain." Still he talks even though she cannot understand. He taps her on the shoulder, turning her slightly in the direction of the door. This much at least is comprehensible, and she leads the way into the old crofter's cottage. Unzipping her coat, she takes it off, a scattering of raindrops splaying across the floor. She moves slowly and uncertainly in the room, aware that furniture may have been added or moved. When she grasps the corner of a chair, she pulls it out, hanging her coat on the back and sitting down at the table.

Gregory shuts the door and sets his rucksack down at the side of the room. He takes her hand to say something, and is surprised by how cold it is. "*Tea?*" She simply nods in response, and he fills up the kettle at the sink before setting it on the floor beside the kitchen's one electricity point, putting the water on the boil.

When he looks up, he sees that she is talking. "*How is Fetlar?*"

"*Good but wet.*" He doesn't speak as quickly or fluidly as she manages, but he finds he can get a reasonable pace now, and the letters come to him easily.

"*It rains everywhere. Did you see the birds?*"

"Yes."

"And what is Fetlar like?"

He is a little taken aback by this question. A Shetlander asking him about their locality. *"Have you never been?"*

"No."

He wonders about this, wonders about how limited her scope of experience actually is. *"Have you ever left Shetland?"*

"I went to Ireland once when I was a little girl. I don't remember a lot. It was very green." She must sense some surprise from him at this comment. *"I wasn't born blind. I could see when I was a child."*

"And you've been on the Shetlands ever since?"

"Yes. I don't travel a lot. Mostly Lunna. Only Lunna these days."

"Why don't..."

"Complicated."

Gregory can imagine it is complicated. Without vision or sound, she is incredibly dependant on the goodwill of others. She cannot transport herself anywhere, an ability that is so essential stuck out here in the wilds. Simple things most people take for granted to the point they don't even consider the issue, like breathing or opening their eyes in the morning. Here Ingrid is living on a farm with parents who do not care to mix. Considering her limited interaction with the world, he is surprised that she is as well educated and eloquent as she is.

He puts two chipped mugs on the table in preparation for the tea. As he is pouring the freshly boiled water, Ingrid abruptly gets up and walks into the makeshift bedroom. Bewildered, Gregory stares after her, setting the kettle on the table. "What's...?"

The sound of a car engine interrupts his pointless question. The noise stops as the ignition is turned off. A pause, then the car door is opened. Who would be visiting him here? He steps up to the window, grimacing as he sees Anna-Mary, warden of Sumburgh Head, taking a waterproof jacket out of the boot of her car. He is quick to change his expression to impersonal pleasantry when she straightens and catches sight of him at the window. He ought not to be so evasive, because she is a nice woman, only a little needy. At least that was the final impression she left with him when they parted in Lerwick, and he has been worried since that she will not leave the matter alone. On the other hand she is supposed to be overseeing the phalarope project, so she is going to be unavoidable for this next year.

He opens the door as Anna-Mary approaches the little croft. The rain has lessened to a light drizzle, weakened and apathetic.

"So this is where you're residing," Anna-Mary says. "Looks very rustic."

"I'm experiencing the full traditional Shetland lifestyle. Do you want to come in?" He glances back into the kitchen, where Ingrid has not returned. It is as if she was never there to begin with.

"Thanks. Oh, you've got the tea on, brilliant." Anna-Mary strides into the kitchen, picking up one of the cups. "I think we must have passed by one another on Fetlar. When I got to Ivan yesterday, he said you'd just left that morning." She abandons the overly-jolly chatter at that point, certain things unsaid as she slurps at Ingrid's tea. Between them is the unspoken understanding that his departure had been more than coincidentally well timed.

"What did you think of Fetlar?"

"Good. Wet but good. It's great habitat for the birds."

"Aye, it's their stronghold on Shetland. Can't do much about the weather though. Although the weatherman reckons we've got a stretch of sunshine coming up – make of that what you may." She strolls idly around the kitchen, taking in the sparse living conditions. Mentally checking through the changes she would make if she were to live here for a year. "Ivan was telling me you think you've found a breeding pair here at Lunna."

"Yep. I've definitely seen them."

"We've not got this on our records. This is good news." She takes another gulp of tea. "You'll have to show me where they are."

"Sure, I can take you up there sometime."

"Now's as good a time as any," Anna-Mary responds. "It's barely spitting now."

Gregory glances through the doorway to his second room. He can't see Ingrid from this angle. Anna-Mary is intruding; he'd be quite content if she left now, but there is a stubbornness about her today – she is going to get something out of this visit. He doesn't feel as though this is the time to introduce the two women. He gestures to the room. "I'll just get my jacket."

"Ivan was telling me it was one of the locals who told you about the birds," Anna-Mary continues as he goes through to the bedroom. "Bit of luck, you happening to stay here."

Ingrid is on a footstool in the corner of the room against the dividing wall to the kitchen. Her face is directed at the floor, and she barely moves when Gregory enters the room. But she must realise that someone has come in, or rather that he is there, because she raises her hands and quickly signs to him. "*I'm not here.*"

It saves him awkward conversations and introductions. He falters, wanting to say something, give a response that he has heard her, but without saying something – which would be pointless – or going to the corner of the room which might make Anna-Mary wonder what he was taking so long over, there isn't much he can do.

"Ivan was telling me that it's some disabled woman," Anna-Mary is still talking when Gregory goes back to the kitchen. "Some kind of cripple," she continues. "Blind, deaf and all sorts. Sounds like a rough way to live."

"Yes. It's impressive the way people adapt," Gregory says, non-committal. He doesn't like the way she is referring to Ingrid as 'some kind of cripple'. It is dismissive, as if she is not a proper person. He almost goes back to the bedroom, wanting to drag her out to show Anna-Mary, regardless of what she might assume of him bringing a blind woman out of his room. She may be deaf, blind and mute, but she is more attune to her surroundings than either of them are. She walks alone and unaided on this land, Gregory thinks; she knew where the birds were, and she knew you were arriving at the cottage before I did. He shrugs on his raincoat. "Shall we go find these birds?"

It takes time, until the afternoon, before Anna-Mary is satisfied she has got all she will for the day, and announces she has to drive back to Sumburgh Head. They have been out to the loch, seen the birds, then headed back to Gregory's croft, where she invites herself for a simple lunch. Upon their return, Gregory cautiously looks into the bedroom, but Ingrid has gone, probably having departed shortly after they had set out for the birds. Now that Anna-Mary has left, he feels he wants to continue the conversation with Ingrid – hadn't she made some comment that she essentially never leaves Lunna? But she is gone and he is not sure where she is. Assumedly somewhere on the farm property, a place where he is not inclined to go. He toys with the idea of not bothering, waiting for her to come here again; either that or bump into her somewhere on the land; but eventually settles on decisive action and sets out for the Jameson farmhouse.

Only the truck is parked outside the farmhouse this afternoon. The yard behind the main building is filled with the sound of bleating lambs from the surrounding fields, and the static-hued noise of the latest chart toppers played on a radio inside. The front door is open at a crack. Gregory steps up to the building, tapping on the door. One of the Jamesons other than Ingrid must be here, because the radio is playing.

"Is that you, mother?" A slightly irritated voice calls from inside.

Shea, Gregory thinks, with a sinking sensation. The swearing, angry little teenager. "It's just me," he responds, pushing the door open and stepping into the front entrance. The kitchen door is wide open, and he has a direct view through to the range, the heavy old oak kitchen table in front.

Shea is standing, a hairbrush in hand. "Oh, it's you," she says.

Gregory steps into the kitchen doorway. "I was just looking for..." he stops as the spread of the kitchen opens up, and he sees Ingrid serenely sitting on a kitchen chair, her profile facing him. She makes no sign that she knows he is there, if she is actually even aware of the fact.

"You wanting a word with my mother?" Shea asks.

"No."

"Pa?"

"No."

She cracks a curious smile. "I see. Grab a pew. I've just got to finish up here."

Gregory walks into the room and sits down in the window seat. Ingrid's back is now facing him. There is a low burning fire crackling in the grate. Shea stands, legs akimbo, her bony hips straining against her tight, hipster jeans, and returns to brushing Ingrid's hair. She is quiet for a moment, eyes downcast with childish concentration. The fact that her own hair has been bunched up in springing, high set pigtails does nothing to pull her away from the immature figure she is so clearly desperate to escape.

"Getting boring on your tod up in the croft?" Shea asks as she draws the hairbrush through the full length of Ingrid's hair.

This is quite a change from the swearing, aggressive little monster he met a few weeks ago when Andrew was still up here. Shea is positively trying to be nice, a coy little smile curling over her lips.

"I don't mind the solitude most of the time."

"But you thought you'd come over and see me for a change."

"I came over to see your sister."

"Ingrid?" Shea sounds mildly disgusted by the suggestion. She stops brushing her hair and looks sharply at Gregory, assuming a stance as if she is preparing to lob the hairbrush in his direction. "What the hell do you want to see Ingrid for? She can't talk, you know."

"I know some sign language."

"Oh, Jesus," Shea rolls her eyes. Slamming the hairbrush on the table, she walks around to stand in front of Ingrid. "We're not finished yet, you know." She unzips a vanity case that is on the table, and starts to rummage through the contents, the clink of plastic bottles and tubs. She takes out a compact of something Gregory can't see from where he is sitting. "Now," she says, looking down at Ingrid, knowing full well she can't hear her. "Let's make you look beautiful."

Shea applies make up to Ingrid's face, playing at make up artist and pointedly ignoring Gregory for a few minutes. "You know what," she abruptly starts up again, at first not clear who she is talking to, even though it is pointless speaking orally to Ingrid. "I don't know why you want to talk to Ingrid. What's she got to talk about?" She pauses, snapping the lid of a lipstick back on. She glares at Gregory. "She's a bit simple, you know."

"How often do you actually talk to your sister?" he asks, surprised by how angry he sounds.

"How often do I talk to my sister?" she repeats, the volume in her voice rising. "What fucking business is it of yours what goes on in our family?" She throws the lipstick hotly into the vanity case. "You need to keep your bloody nose out." She zips up the vanity case, collecting her belongings. Her face contorts into another scowl. "Retard." She mutters, not clear if the insult is meant for Ingrid or Gregory, before she marches huffily out of the kitchen.

There is a moment of silence; Gregory still taken aback by Shea's little performance. Ingrid shifts slightly, then pushes her chair back, standing up. She turns, and Gregory visibly winces, thinking afterwards that it is a good thing she is blind and cannot see his expression. She looks garish, like a pantomime dame, with bright aquamarine eye shadow all the way up to her eyebrows, a bright red mouth, painted beyond the natural contours of her lips so that her mouth takes on a ridiculous, cartoonish quality. She has two thick circles of pink blusher, as if she is a wooden puppet.

"*Hello.*"

So she knows that he is in the room.

"*I have to wash my face.*"

There's an understatement, Gregory thinks, wondering why she lets Shea do this to her.

"*Do I look like a mess?*"

Gregory stands up and takes her hand. "*It's not flattering.*"

"*She was in a bad mood.*"

Ingrid walks out into the entrance hallway, and Gregory moves to sit back into the window seat to wait for her to wash up. She pauses, then turns back to the kitchen doorway.

"*I don't live here.*"

"You don't?" Gregory asks, rhetorically, vocally, pointlessly.

"*Come with me.*"

Ingrid leads the way out of the house and across the yard to the barn. At one end of the barn there is a small door, easily overlooked. It opens onto a staircase to the first floor. Gregory follows her, horrified to think that her parents keep her in the rafters of the barn, a secret from the island, shunned away even from her own family. He is impressively surprised to discover that the first floor of the barn has been renovated into a modern studio apartment, high rectangular windows allowing warm sunlight through to flow along the wooden flooring. There's a settee, a couple of desks and chairs, the walls along underneath the windows all lined with packed bookcases. At the far end there is a large bed, a wardrobe and a chest of drawers. In the space closest to the staircase, there is a neatly laid out kitchen – in fact everything is carefully planned, no doubt matching the mental image Ingrid has of her retreat so that she can easily navigate herself through her home. She opens a door at the side of the kitchen which reveals a brightly tiled bathroom.

"*I have to clean my face*," she repeats, before disappearing inside, leaving Gregory to wonder at her little flat.

This is where Ingrid lives, exists, to the point where she is a virtual prisoner; only able to wander her family's farmlands. Why did she never leave – surely there must be better facilities for people with her disabilities on the mainland. Perhaps she didn't want to leave Shetland. Gregory walks silently through the main living area, gazing at the rows and rows of books, each with a Braille title running down the spine. Assumedly all in English, yet all completely inaccessible to him.

There are two desks in this section. One is cluttered, clearly where she works. There is surprisingly a full computer terminal, as he is used to, with a rather hi tech looking printer. There's some printed sheets on stacking trays beside it; or rather punched paper; the neat rows of dots pushed out, marking out the touch-based form of reading. Gregory runs a rough finger over the top of the sheet. The dots are perceptible, but how the hell can someone make enough sense of these indentations to get words and sentences? In front of the computer terminal, set neatly on the wooden desk, there is a largish flat black plastic box, with a cable snaking back across to the processing unit. In the top surface of the box there are a great number of small holes, all regularly spaced. From the gloom of the holes, he can see little white pointers, perhaps dull lumps that can come up and protrude from the holes. Like a miniature version of that children's game, hit the head of the creature as it dares to peek out from the holes. One could form sentences of Braille words on this box. He looks back at the computer screen, rather pointlessly set on a desk in Ingrid's flat. Perhaps this box is her way of seeing the screen.

He walks over to the other desk, where a small typewriter is set. He draws out the chair from the desk and sits in front of the machine, assuming this is more familiar. He could not write a word on this machine, in fact it looks more like an old fashioned cash register. At the top there are a couple of slots for the paper to come in and out of the machine, with flick switches to adjust position and hold the paper in place. On the front where Gregory would expect to find the alphabet, there is only one row of seven push-down shelves, with two smaller, darker ones set higher up, one to each side. The central button in the line of seven is a larger, elongated button.

The bathroom door opens and Ingrid appears, fresh face and no longer looking like a poorly made up night club drag queen. She pauses in the room, her hands by her sides, fingers splayed out a little as if uncertain where to go. This is her territory, and although she cannot see it, she had a mental image, knowing where every item is, how many steps and in which direction, how far she can swing her arm out before she will hit a certain piece of furniture. Yet she hesitates, and Gregory realises that although she knows he is in the room, whether by assuming he didn't leave, or by some acute, developed sense; she is not sure exactly where he is.

She starts to walk through the centre of the room. He hates to use the terminology, but as a normal person would walk through a room – an easy confident pace, able to judge the depth, distance and spacing between objects. She holds her hands out at her side in a subtle sensory pose, and when she comes to the desks, he reaches out and touches her arm so that she knows he is sitting at her desk. She stops and turns, reaching out to his shoulder, perhaps making certain she has judged correctly when assuming he is sitting down.

"Do I look sane now?"

"Much better." He pauses, still distracted by catching sight of small details of her flat, physical representations of her mind, her personality. *"This flat is a surprise."*

"Really?"

"It just looks like a barn from the outside."

"It is still a barn downstairs." She moves fluidly, stepping around to the opposite side of the desk, a blind hand reaching out and taking the back of a chair she knew would be there, drawing it around so that they can sit face to face. *"They accepted I needed my own space, and renovated the first floor for me. I've had this over ten years now. It's possible to make a good renovation with a little time. Doesn't have to be as basic as your croft."*

Gregory smiles wryly. With time anything can be made good. She certainly doesn't slum it here, with her own fully fitted little corner kitchen, a bathroom with running water – hot and cold; proper heating, proper comfortable furniture. *"It's very nice."*

She gives a little nod. *"I couldn't cope in your croft. Especially in the winter."*

Something he has yet to experience, he thinks grimly.

"If you get tired of the cold and want hot water, you can come here." She offers. *"Use the kitchen, the shower. It's not a problem; I'm blind, you know."* She adds as a little joke.

"Thank you. I may take you up on that offer." Someone had mentioned to him early on that he could come up to the farmhouse to borrow the conveniences. He had not felt inclined, instead telling himself he'd rather wash with the cold water of the croft, even if it meant having to crack the ice off the surface on a morning in winter. Big words for a modern age used to central heating. The farmhouse is not a welcoming place, however, this secret little flat in the barn is comfortable, like a sanctuary against the silence and the biting sea winds.

Ingrid puts her hands out on the table, running her fingers up the side of the odd looking typewriter. *"This is my Perkins typewriter. I don't use it very much now as I have the computer. But I used this all the time when I was younger."*

"It's strange. Not many keys."

"It's to type Braille. Braille is just dots on paper. There's only so many positions you can put a dot, so you don't need many keys."

Being blind is like having to learn another language, just as being deaf is, Gregory reflects. Having to learn an entirely new writing form. He watches her hands drift back down the sides of the Braille typewriter. Her fingers must be incredibly sensitive; to be able to perceive the words and sentences punched into pieces of paper. The way she perceives the world around her, how she can interact, communicate, take part and learn. He wonders if her brain somehow translates what she senses into a mental image in her mind's eye. For she must have a vague memory of colours, forms, shapes, from her childhood before she lost her sight. Even now, sitting directly in front of her, her pupiless eyes staring directly at him, he can't help but feel as though she can actually see him, is watching, and knows of everything that is happening around her.

When Gregory first came to Shetland, first met the Jameson family, he was quite sure he would spend little to no time at the farm, and certainly none in the Jamesons' company. The past week has proved to be a considerable u-turn, and a standstill as far as his work is concerned.

The usual morning walks, bird watching and revelling in the peace continue, as does Ingrid's company. This association now extends to evenings in the warmth and comfort of her barn-studio flat. Being welcomed into someone's home is to discover who they really are as a person. Just as the old saying that you never really know someone until you live with them goes.

Ingrid has continued to offer up a number of surprises, crumbling the few remaining preconceptions he had over her disabilities. For instance, Ingrid 'listens' to music – not in the conventional sense, but she can feel the vibrations and appreciate a rhythm. Drum and bass as a genre, and generally tracks with drumming or bass guitar are particular favourites; Ingrid appreciates a certain resonance that the hearing music-loving community perhaps overlook. It is often said that the percussion; the bass guitarists and musicians providing the canvas for the other instruments to play on are often underappreciated. Gregory wonders if perhaps they have missed their target fan club – the deaf.

Ingrid plays card games with an adapted pack that have the numbers and suits embossed. She has a surprisingly wide knowledge of different games (Gregory suspects she's spent a lot of long, dull evenings learning these things in the hope that one day she might have company). She also has a scrabble set that has been painstakingly adapted by hand, with the Braille counterpart of the letters with transparent blobs of varnish. All of these sets are underused, and for all the hours he is in her flat, there is no interruption of any description from her family. Ingrid prepares most of her own meals in her kitchen, and to all intents and purposes, lives as though she has long flown the nest, independent and free.

Aside from studying (another perpetual student in the family) she also earns a small income writing articles for blind and deaf-blind publications, and also some articles on Shetland history for publications aimed at the seeing community – this has only been possible since the advent of the internet and email. Prior to this technology communication between the seeing and the blind was awkward. Ingrid might have been able to print off an article in regular print from her own computer, but it was very difficult for any editorial team to communicate to her without having to use costly translation services, getting letters and notes into Braille. Occasionally her mother had helped, reading some letters to her, an aside that surprises Gregory as Eilidh has not struck him as particularly interested in her daughter.

By the end of the week, he is aware that his own work has stagnated, and decides he needs to start exploring the islands. Summer is warming up the intense green of the islands. He will have to spend a couple of weeks camping his way around the island to get the backbone of research complete for his writing. When he mentions this to Ingrid on the way back towards the croft, she grows irritated and non-responsive, and he comes upon a spontaneous idea, an extension of the plans he'd already made for the day.

"I'm going on a day trip today. You should come with me."

"Leave the farm?" An overall sense of horror radiates from her body language.

"Yes, it will do you good." He unlocks the car and opens the passenger door.

"No. I can't." She turns and starts to walk away, aware that Gregory no longer can see her hands, stuffed into her pockets. Communication is turned off.

When she says she's not left Lunna for a long time, he wonders if it's a case of can't or won't. Leaving the familiar isn't as simple for Ingrid as it is for other people, but since getting to know her, he can see that she lets her disabilities hinder her as little possible. He won't let a little nervousness stop his idea from fruitition. He strides after her, catching her by the shoulders and redirecting her to the car. Ingrid's pace slows, it does not stop completely, but she shrinks into herself at the enormity of the big wide world.

"I'm going to somewhere I want to write about in the book."

"Not Lerwick?"

"No."

She stops beside the car, appearing to seriously consider the possibility, although she is genuinely worried. It's the first time he's seen any lack of confidence from Ingrid. She turns to him. *"You won't leave me anywhere?"*

He looks at her, utterly bemused. What does she think of him? Or what does she think goes on out there beyond the boundaries of Lunna? *"I'm not going to pull a practical joke on you."*

Ingrid's shoulders sag. *"Sorry."* Her fingers hover, paused. *"It's just..."*

"Let's have a change of scene."

"Where?"

"Surprise."

Everything considered Ingrid sits reasonably calmly in the passenger seat for the hour it takes Gregory to drive to his chosen destination. She has to open the window for fresh air, grimacing a little, and making some sign of motion sickness. If she's hardly ever left Lunna in recent years, she won't be used to travelling in a car. He wonders if this has been a good idea, but continues regardless, convincing himself it will be worth it when they arrive and she can put her feet back on steady land again.

After turning off the main road, the spine of mainland Shetland, he is back on single tracked lanes, sloping downwards towards the sea. The route eventually peters out into a rudimentary gravel car park lined by a chicken wire fence post and a view across the sea. Gregory turns the engine off and gets out of the car, walking to the passenger side to open the door. Ingrid looks pensive, jumping at the sound of the door being pulled back, the fresh air swooping in towards her. She clips off the seatbelt and swings around to put her feet outside, moving the soles of her shoes across the surface. Relatively flat, loose stones. She can smell salt in the air. The breeze is fresh.

"I've brought my stick," she signs.

"Your stick?" Gregory mutters, really for himself, not feeling a need to sign it to her. She hadn't brought anything with her, only herself, her jacket."

"It's telescopic," Ingrid continues as if having guessed he would not understand, patting her jacket pocket in a pause in her speech. *"But I don't want to have to use it."* She stands up slowly, her

normal grace and ease gone. Gregory watches, realising he perhaps hasn't appreciated just how debilitated she really is. Her confidence at Lunna is misleading. It almost makes one forget that she is blind.

He offers her his hand, but she quickly moves up his arm, linking arms as if bolting onto him. She will not be walking anywhere he isn't going, no chance of being abandoned in this silent, great sightless unknown before her. She can feel the scrunching gravel beneath her feet, a sea breeze coming over some kind of low-lying obstruction or windbreak to the side, and the sunshine on the top of her head. They walk to the end of the car park and along the path to the shore. The ground surface turns to soft, dry sand; Ingrid feels the slip of each tread, as the sand gives way, leaving a hollow mark where she has just passed. Then they are down to the shore, on the flat, hard packed wet sand.

"Where are we?"

"St Ninian's Isle; on the tombolo."

She grins and clutches onto his arm more tightly. *"I remember. We came here in primary; before I lost my sight."*

St Ninian's Isle is walkable from the mainland most of the time, except for extreme high spring tides. A grassy island with scenic cliffs, breeding seabirds in the late spring, and only the memory of human habitation; a site of a great treasure find by a schoolboy. The connection between the island and the mainland is a tombolo, a machair of white sands, created by the sea itself as it surged around the island from both ends, pushing up mounds of sand to meet at a point in the middle, creating a permanent walk way of beach out to the island. When the sun shines, as it does now, the water is an exquisite turquoise shade, looking almost tropical. The colours here are vivid, from the bright green fields and grasslands, right up to the bright skies.

They walk up one edge of the beach, skirting along the front of the dunes at the start of the island, then turn and walk down the other side of the beach. There are not many other tourists, a couple of walkers who are straight off up onto the island to take a circular walk around the various cliffs and views. Ingrid gradually grows in confidence, breaking free of Gregory to gingerly step to the edge of the beach, a little too far and the incoming tide washes over her shoes, drenching her socks. She seems to be thrilled by this, and crouches down to put her hands to the water, waiting for the next wave to break. Although Shetland is made up of crumpled coastlines that journey back and forth upon themselves, much of it is rocky with imposing cliffs, and these sections of clean sand spreads dotted around the islands are real treats. There is nothing like this at the farm. They sit on the dune slopes of wind-dry sand and talk, intermittent as Ingrid savours delving her hands into the sand, the coolness underneath the surface and the willingness to part when she pushes against it.

Walking around an unknown island with so many sheer drops isn't really a possibility as Ingrid will have to move so slowly to be sure she doesn't misplace a step. She is happy to sit on the beach, to be somewhere she has not been for twenty years, to recall distant memories of sight and sound, a childhood before things started to break down. When they agree it's time to leave the island, she is adamant she wants to go directly back to Lunna. She is hoping that no one has noticed her absence, Gregory thinks. She refuses to go anywhere there will be people in any great number. He's a little disappointed that the adventure should end so quickly, but reminds himself that this is probably the first time in years she has left her comfort zone of Lunna. This is going to take time. On the next trip they shall be a little more adventurous.

It had developed as what appeared to be a good idea. In fact Gregory had congratulated himself for a week on this stroke of cunning plotting. Had he realised what would happen in his absence, he wouldn't have gone away, but retrospect and hindsight are luxuries mere mortals don't enjoy.

He has been away for a week, travelling and camping around Unst, researching for the guidebook. Before departing, he had told Ingrid that he would be going away, the news of which had provoked a rather depressive response. Even her mood hadn't deterred him, as he had thought it would only contribute to his ultimate plan. He'd driven off with foolish, perhaps schoolboyish ideas, that the trip to St Ninian's, coupled with his week's absence, would encourage her to bravery, and that by the height of summer she'd come away travelling the islands with him.

Now he admits that his imagination had gotten the better of him. Ingrid isn't a pet dog to trot loyally at his heels where ever he goes. Neither is she some romantic interest, a summer fling or elongated holiday girlfriend – there is a certain kind of innocence about her, perhaps projected by his preconceived ideas about handicapped people. Whatever it is, casual flings should be conducted on level territory, and in this situation it is unthinkable, taking advantage of a vulnerable person. The more he thinks about this potential aspect with Ingrid, the less he knows what to think. As it transpires, Ingrid's own actions for that week apart solve any dilemma over casual involvements and rendez vous.

Gregory returns to the croft mid morning. Already as he is unpacking the car he is keen to see Ingrid, half an eye on the path down from the fields, hoping for her to come strolling down, as if she has sensed the vibrations of a particular car engine and will come rushing to be reunited with her friend. He eats a quick lunch, takes a walk around the farm, checks on the phalaropes and their chicks, but doesn't bump into Ingrid.

Over recent weeks, they have developed an understanding about one another's company, and she is quite relaxed for him to turn up unannounced at her little flat whenever the notion strikes him. He is always amused by the fact that she never seems surprised when he arrives, having to touch her shoulder to announce his arrival. The door to the flat is never locked and he can go straight up. Except this time things are different. The door is locked.

Gregory tests the handle a second time, doubting himself. It is definitely locked. He steps back from the barn, looking up at the windows and for a moment forgets himself and thinks to shout up to her. But of course that is pointless; she wouldn't hear.

The door to the main farmhouse opens and the sheepdog belts out as if escaping a fire. The animal charges straight for Gregory, having already sensed he was on the property, and has his front paws on Gregory's legs, straining up for attention.

"Seamus!" Eilidh scolds as she also leaves the building, grumpily carrying a plastic box full of items, flinging it rather unceremoniously into the back of her car.

The dog drops to all fours and looks sheepishly at the ground before trotting back over to the matriarch, tail hung low.

"Mrs Jameson," Gregory starts, striding in her direction.

Eilidh turns sharply, staring coldly at him. "Am I to assume you're looking for Ingrid?" she asks, although they both know the answer. She regards him, as if accusing him of mischief. "She's not here."

"Where is she?"

"She's gone to the mainland."

"The mainland?" For a moment he isn't sure what she is referring to. Lunna is technically part of the Shetland mainland – surely the locals of Lunna can't consider themselves separate from it? Then he realises what she means – the mainland of the UK. This is surreal. Ingrid hasn't left Lunna in years; St Ninian was an adventure that almost pushed her boundaries too far. Aside from all the impossibilities, she didn't mention this to him a week ago.

Eilidh slams the back door of her car shut. "Shea's taken her. She won't be back for months."

"I'm sorry, I don't..."

"Oh for goodness sake," Eilidh snaps. "She's gone for surgery. She'll either have months of rehabilitation or she'll be left a dribbling idiot. Anyway, I thought you had a book to write and wildlife to watch. That's why you're here isn't it? You won't have to worry about entertaining the charity case now, will you?"

Gregory feels a bitterness in his stomach turn over. Eilidh is a cold, matter-of-fact mother, even with mortality in the shadows. He watches as she marches around to the driver's door, then stops and looks back at him. She reads his expression, and nods slightly to herself, as if pleased with the response she has provoked, and relents a little in her attitude.

"Where is she?"

"At the hospital." She pauses, her arm resting across the top of the open car door. "Does it matter? You can't talk to her on the phone; you can't write her a note. She made a conscious decision not to tell you when you headed off last week. Now, I've got to get to work, so I'll bid you good day."

Gregory stands dumbly in the middle of the farmyard, Seamus the dog laid upon the doorstep, as Eilidh swings the car around and drives off down the road. Gone. And what little life there had been at the farm has now vanished, with no promise of ever coming back.

During the next three months, the bulk of the summer, Gregory spends little time at Lunna. He decides that whilst the weather is good, it is time to conduct the bulk of the work. When winter sets in, he can sit down and write. And not necessarily at Lunna. Although the original rose-tinted ideal had been to disappear to a remote shack on Shetland for a year, this has grown less appealing of late, despite the arrival of summer. The winter will be long, dark, cold and damp with little to no company. He toys with the idea of moving to somewhere a little more modernised for the winter, but makes no definite plans as of yet.

He hears nothing of Ingrid. Eilidh is illusive, and after asking a couple of times without any real answer, he gives up. He has no method of contact, and must accept that this has been decided and this is what she wanted. As much as he grew to like Ingrid, she is still a Jameson in her heart and they are a strange family. Determined not to connect with the outside world.

A few days after Ingrid's sudden departure, Gregory bumps into Jayne Castleton, wife of local sheep farmer. She jests that he is a dark horse, something of a ladies' man. First the Norwegian tourist – yes, of course they all noticed that he didn't leave the guesthouse until the following morning – and then a mysterious red head in his car the other week. They must mean Ingrid. Hugo Castleton, one of John Jameson's compatriots in the local farming industry, had seen Gregory driving back home with Ingrid. He hadn't recognised Ingrid – in fact no one outside the Jameson circle has any notion of who she might be. Gregory feels as though he has agreed to keep a secret no one has explained to him. He makes light of Jayne's prying teasing, with some vague fictional explanation for who the red head is.

For his work, he covers a lot of ground during those months, exploring the mainland and outlying tiny islands such as St Ninian's and Mousa. Then onwards to the major islands: Yell, Unst and Fetlar set to the north of the mainland; Whalsey, the Out Skerries, Bressay and Noss to the east; and Papa Stour and Foula with its famous towering sea cliffs to the west. He takes another trip to Fair

Isle, the far flung island to the south, famous for the seabirds and knitting patterns. Whilst the constant travel and exploration is enjoyable, living cheaply camping, and at hostels, meeting new people every day, mostly tourists, it is good to have conversation of longer standing, and the same bed and room to inhabit for several days in a row. He is staying at Alan Brun's house on Fair Isle. Alan is an old university colleague who left ambitions, career and fast living to come and run the bird station on this tiny island out in the wind-battered seas.

Gregory leans against the long row of windows, bottle of beer in one hand, as he looks out to the sea. Fog is building out on the open water and creeping towards the land. He'd heard on the radio that the next couple of days were not going to be particularly good. Thick fog, low visibility – perhaps this doesn't matter so much, for Fair Isle is not a big place. But it does not do to accidentally wander off a cliff due to low visibility, and it must be disappointing for the tourists who have come across as part of their week's holiday in Shetland. This was their one opportunity to see the birds and experience the uplifting isolation.

"Have you been across to Mousa at night yet?"

Gregory shifts his gaze away from the sea, to Alan, who is hunched forward in a stiff-backed, second-hand armchair. "Not yet. I keep meaning to."

"You have all the time in the world. At least it seems that way. You'll have to get yourself over there. It's something to see, with all the wee birds flying back to the nest." He stops, mid-thought, as his mobile phone buzzes. He reads the text message, not particularly surprised, but reading through it twice to be sure of the content. "Libby's not coming back over from the mainland tomorrow."

"Is this the woman you're seeing at the moment?"

Alan sighs. "Aye." He turns the mobile phone face down and places it on the table as if he wants no more to do with the world for today. "It's never simple, is it? Anyway, tell me, how are you getting on at Lunna? I don't suppose you'll have been there that much recently."

"Barely. I'm getting the bulk of the research done now. It's a nice enough place, certainly for the solitude. It has a certain atmosphere."

"That'll be the trowies."

Gregory smiles lightly. "That or the Jamesons."

"Yeah, you can certainly understand why Andrew is the way he is," Alan laughs. "They're a funny bunch, even for farmers. I remember one of my father's old girlfriends having a few run ins with Eilidh when she was working up there. Eilidh left her in the lurch in the end."

Alan is a few years older than Andrew Jameson, but as a fellow Shetlander, they are aware of one another from the homeland, as well as later connections at the university.

"You ever meet Ingrid?" Gregory asks him. It sounds like an idle question, just a way to make conversation, but even the utterance of her name is heavily loaded. Alan is a rational, calm man, who knows a lot about the islands, more than most. It would be good to get a second opinion, for the more Gregory has thought over everything about Ingrid, the more illogical it all seems. Something is wrong.

"Andrew's younger sister? Well, not the wee tart they had a lot later," Alan concedes, referring to Shea. "I must have met her I suppose, although I don't remember having much to do with her."

"I suppose with her dying at primary school..." Gregory broaches one of the popular myths surrounding Ingrid.

"Primary school? No, you've been listening to local gossip. They had to pull her out of primary school over night; I think that's why people reckon she died suddenly, but it didn't happen like that."

"So she's not dead?"

"Ach, no, she's dead now, or at least I think so." He pauses. "She must be, but it happened a few years later, in her early teens. She wasn't a well wee lassie, probably was dying for years. She woke up blind one day, that's why they took her out of school. There wasn't really anywhere set up to deal with that. They had her homeschooled, this woman came up from the mainland – just out of university, you know, looking to prove her worth. My dad went out with her for a bit; this is how I know. I think she did pretty well, teaching her Braille, getting her used to the new way of dealing with the world. She taught her for a few years, then turned up at the farm one day and Eilidh told her that her services were no longer required, just like that, no more work. Eilidh was going to do the homeschooling now, she said. Wouldn't even let her say goodbye to the lass. It wasn't handled very well at all."

"And you think she died just after that?"

"I guess so." Alan gives him a sly look. "What have the locals round Lunna been telling you?"

"Nothing. Everyone seems to think she's dead."

"Seems to think? You're not suggesting she's still alive?"

"She is. I've met her."

"My mother didn't knit me," Alan laughs. "Ingrid Jameson is still alive but the whole of Shetland thinks she's dead? Come off it. You've been seeing a few wee ghosties. It's the atmosphere up there you know; Lunna's a funny place."

"I'm not joking with you. She lives up there on the farm; they've made her a flat above one of the barns. She's deaf-blind and mute, but gets about on the property surprisingly well. But everyone thinks she's dead. The locals at Lunna don't know about her. I went out with her one day, and they saw her in my car and were all wondering who she was – they had no idea. It's weird; it feels like this great unmentioned secret."

"You're being serious."

"Of course I am. Then something strange happened a couple of months ago. She'd told me that she'd not left the farm for a long long time."

"How can she tell you that? You just said she's deaf and blind."

"And mute. There's an adapted sign language you can use for deaf-blind. She wouldn't say why; but then suddenly one day she's gone. Not just from the farm but the islands. Eilidh said she's gone to the mainland, but wouldn't tell me where. And I've heard nothing since."

The mood in the room has taken on a sombre, thoughtful aspect. Alan digests this information, slowly nursing his beer. "That sounds bloody weird," he finally agrees. "I know Eilidh Jameson's always been a bit of a control freak – she's a scary woman, but I'm sure you don't need me to tell you that. Funny though, because she lets Shea run wild. I wonder what she thinks she's protecting Ingrid from. Shit, to have been kept hidden from the world since your teens on that farm? She must be some undeveloped freak."

"That's part of the strangeness. She's not. She's very intelligent, quite normal. The most likeable of the entire family."

"I really should have come over to the mainland a different day," Alan considers, a little too late as the mail boat from Fair Isle is pulling into Lerwick harbour. "Once a fortnight it comes to Lerwick, that's it. I need to be down at Sumburgh."

"Quit your moaning. You know my car's parked at the terminal. I'll give you a lift down to Sumburgh. I really should go myself. Got a lot of work to do for the RSBP."

"I need to see Anna-Mary too. Nip into base camp, then that's me away on a plane to Scotland."

"I thought we already were in Scotland."

"You know what I mean."

The mail boat, one of two ways to get to Fair Isle, is dwarfed in the harbour by the ferry shipping, destinations Aberdeen, Torshavn, Bergen. In such a boat, every movement is magnified. Gregory remained out in the air for the entire journey, thankful it was only to be a couple of hours. Although he'd flown out to the island from Tingwall, he'd thought he'd save a few pounds and come back on the mail boat. He was trying to be economical with his money. It was always easy to be economical when you weren't trying to hold down the sense of impending vomit, trying to look tough in front of your friends. At least now his feet are back on steady land, his stomach can get control over itself again.

Heading towards the main ferry terminal, in the direction of Gregory's car, they approach as some passengers from Aberdeen are leaving the ship at the last moment, having enjoyed a lazy breakfast on board the moored vessel. Alan nods towards a figure laden down with a heavy rucksack. "That's Shea Jameson, isn't it?"

Gregory scans over the figures, soon noting the roughly dyed pink hair, the tight jeans, and general angry demeanour that is Shea. "Looks like her," he admits, noting that the girl appears to be alone.

"I still can't believe what you told me the other evening; that Ingrid's still alive."

"It's true," Gregory says vaguely, watching Shea stumble about. At least it was the truth a few months ago, the last time I saw her, he thinks. Perhaps Eilidh has done away with her since and concocted a tale of going to the mainland.

As they near each other, Shea happens to turn and catch sight of him. She scowls as an immediate, unconscious reaction, before something occurs to her and she lightens her attitude, trying to be pleasant, nodding to him. "Gregory," she says, as if they are old friends. "I didn't see you on the boat from Aberdeen."

"That's because I wasn't on it."

He can see she is struggling to keep her smart mouth in check; she wants something and it wouldn't do to be rude.

"Are you heading up to Lunna now?"

There it is. A lift. Strange how many of the Jameson family he has driven about on the island. Gregory shakes his head. "I'm going down to Sumburgh."

"Well, that was a waste of time," Shea growls to no one in particular, already scanning the passersby for a potential free ride.

"How's your sister?"

She jumps at this question, looks suspiciously at Gregory, then at Alan, who has also stopped. They must know each other. "What, you mean Ingrid? Have you been talking to him about her?"

"Jesus, she really is alive," Alan can't help himself.

Shea glares at him as if he is a moron. "No one ever said she was dead," she snaps, followed by an 'arsehole' that is barely audible.

The unofficial secret, Gregory thinks. No one will out and out lie about Ingrid, but it's something that shouldn't be spoken of; if people assume with time that she is dead, then all the better. "So how is she?"

"Don't you know? Living it up in Edinburgh, playing catch the ball whilst that moron doctor makes puppy eyes at her. I bet he ends up marrying her."

"I thought your mother said she was going to hospital."

"Yeah, that's where doctors work." Shea tells him in a droning teenage voice, typical of the thirteen to sixteen bracket, usually accompanied by a little eye rolling and generally gormless expression. All to denote that you, not them, are the idiot. "It's all fine; they operated, got the tumour out..."

"Tumour?" Gregory interrupts. He hadn't realised Ingrid's health was that seriously affected.

"It wasn't cancer. Just a lump in her head. I thought they usually called that her brain," she sniggers. "You don't need to look so freaked. She's not dying. Unfortunately."

Alan is a little bemused. "This is your older sister we're talking about?"

"She's a lying bitch."

"Shea, what..."

"Yeah, so you know she's got her sight back since they took out this tumour. It was pressing on her optic nerves or something. But the doctor can't cure her hearing, and do you know why?"

Shea's face is a riddle. Gregory isn't sure whether she's about to burst into tears or start kicking his shins. She probably doesn't know herself. She's angry, but that's just the cover to something more complicated going on underneath. "I don't know," he responds calmly. "Irreparable damage?"

"She's not deaf. She never was. She's not mute either; she just chooses not to speak to us." She looks pleased with the reaction it gets from him. "My entire life she's been pretending she can't hear me. She's been eavesdropping on our conversations all these years, playing the dumb arse. She is such a selfish, back stabbing bitch."

Gregory is flicking back through his memories of Ingrid, looking for a sign, a moment when it didn't fit. He can't think of an episode when she has responded to sound, made any sign that she has heard him. For although he has always known she is deaf, he couldn't help himself, talking an unconscious, automatic action. Can it be true? Perhaps this is just one of Shea's strange attacks on her sister. But if it is true, suddenly Ingrid has become a different person, a being that can see, hear, speak. A being that one is allowed to mention in front of strangers, not a secret to hide away on the farm. "Is she coming back?"

Shea sticks her thumbs under the shoulder straps of her rucksack, as if to take the strain better. "I don't know. I hope not. That lying cow can go rot."

The two men stand, dust settling after a tornado, as Shea stomps away towards town. Alan looks over at Gregory. "Jesus." He is the first to break the silence. "It's all kicking off since you moved up here. First you tell me dead little Ingrid's still alive; and now she's got her sight back? If she comes back to Shetland, I'm coming up to Lunna for a visit."

"Yeah, sure," Gregory mutters. With this update of events, Ingrid has become a stranger to him. Odd, but he's not sure how much he is looking forward to the possibility of seeing her again either.

On a wire suspended above a low wall, a wren is perched, its head bobbing frantically from one angle to the next, as small birds do, examining the immediate area, thinking of food and somewhere warm to sleep tonight. The wind blows around the corner of the building and whips up the bird's feathers, showing just how fluffed up its plumage is, and how fragile a tiny beast it is.

Gregory is sitting in front of a PC, but he is not doing any work. He has given up the pretext of staring at the screen. He wants this work finished so that he does not have to come here again, but his mind has gone as blank as the screen saver in front of him. A radio is humming deeper in the office, coupled with the sound of Astrid's steady typing. The summer is over, but she has still not left Sumburgh Head. She'll be heading back to university in Aberdeen next week, and like Gregory, has the notes and reports for the summer project to finalise. The red-necked phalaropes are now long gone, the chicks fledged and away with their parents. Late September, where they find themselves now, is definitely autumn. The days have become noticeably short, and yet this is only part way through the long down-hill roll towards the 21 December when they will endure the shortest day of the year. Mornings are cold, nights are colder, and Gregory's enthusiasm for staying the whole winter on Shetland has waned. As much as he does not enjoy risking Anna-Mary appearing in the room at every opportune moment, he has lapped up the central heating that accommodation at the Sumburgh Head station affords. Romantic notions of rustic accommodation in old cottages are soon extinguished when you are woken up by a chilled hug from the air, and ice on the window panes.

A door bangs as someone enters the building, shuffling in the corridor outside the office. Anna-Mary's voice comes through the open doorway. Astrid looks up from her work. "We have got to get ourselves down to the hotel," she tells the student. "You will not believe what's... oh." The gossiping halts as she enters the room and sees Gregory sat at a computer, at first hidden from sight of the doorway as he is across by the window. "You're still here?"

"I'm almost finished." He would have finished a couple of hours ago had his mind not been wandering.

"Well, it's a good thing," Anna-Mary continues, bustling into the room. "You should have told me."

"Told you what?"

"That Ingrid Jameson's not dead!" Her voice rises in pitch and volume, a slightest twist of the dial. It reveals her irritation, as if he has betrayed her, the moment of foolishness when she had found out this morning at the Sumburgh Head Hotel. "I couldn't believe it when Mark told me. Apparently she went blind when she was younger, so they had to pull her out of school, but she never actually died." She pauses, still staring at Gregory as something occurs to her. "Ivan said some crippled woman at Lunna had told you where the phalaropes at Lunna were. She was blind; that was Ingrid, wasn't it? I remember us sitting here talking about her when you first came to Shetland. And you never said a word about it. I even came over to Lunna – you could have taken me to see her."

Gregory doesn't care for her tone of voice. She sounds angry, sulky, like a child who has been left out of the games, but would like to be everyone's best friend, privy to all the secrets. She feels he has shown disloyalty by not reporting all the particulars of his life at Lunna back to her.

"Well?" Anna-Mary snaps, but her confidence soon cracks when she reads his expression. He isn't a student she can dominate by the rights of age. He will not play school boy to her angry teacher. Astrid raises her eyebrows as she looks from Anna-Mary to Gregory, amused by the standoff.

"Anyway," Anna-Mary breaks the silence first, backing down. "We should head down to the hotel now. There's quite a few people there already."

"What's going on?" Astrid asks.

"She's coming back today. Her flight should be landing in the next half hour or so. They're having a bit of a welcome back lunch at the hotel. It's an open thing, anyone can go."

Astrid looks back to the computer. "Sounds like a bit of a freak show."

At least there is some consideration left in the world, Gregory thinks gratefully, as Astrid makes it quite clear she has no interest in gawking at a blind woman now cured whom she has never met.

"You'll come though, Gregory?" Anna-Mary asks, taking her car keys out of her pocket. "I'm heading back down there now."

Driving and not walking, Gregory thinks – she doesn't want to miss a thing. Part of him wants to say no, simply to be contrary; but he would like to see Ingrid again; find out how she is. The curiosity is too big a pull. "Sure," he eventually agrees. The paperwork will wait until later this afternoon.

The Sumburgh Head Hotel is a grey-stone, stately Victorian gothic building set by the coast at the base of the Sumburgh Head Hill. Only a few metres above sea level, it is surrounded by neat green fields, commanding views across to white sands on the curved bay against a thin strip of land where the road comes down from Lerwick and winds round up to the lighthouse at the very end of the mainland. Beyond the sands is the main airport servicing the islands, where Ingrid will shortly be landing. Just across from the hotel car park is the historic monument Jarlshof – a settlement that has been in existence since the Neolithic, through to the bronze age, the Viking years and up to the medieval period; ruined examples of stone dwellings from each period packed in, one against the other, to create a walk around of the early history of Shetland.

It is only twelve o'clock, outside of the main tourist season, and yet the hotel is busy with people, the atmosphere buzzing, and many look to the door as Gregory and Anna-Mary arrive, disappointed to see that it is no one special. Anna-Mary soon slips into the crowds, having spotted a friend who is waving for her attention, in all probability an update on the gossip. Gregory goes to the bar and orders a pint, feeling uncomfortable. This is surreal, the kind of thing that feels as though it really has nothing what so ever to do with Ingrid. For someone who has spent all of her adult life isolated and had contact with only a handful of people, this may be quite scary.

"Hey, Gregory!" David Henriksson, one of Andrew's friends who had let them crash at his Lerwick flat all those months ago on first arrival in Shetland, is sitting at a window table. Gregory heads over, glad to be retreating to the sidelines, out of the crowds.

"I suppose you'll be the least surprised of us all about today," David starts, as Gregory joins him. "What with you having stayed up at Lunna all these months. You must have known that Ingrid was still alive."

Everyone thought she was dead. There must have been countless opportunities when the family could have corrected this – either by a slip of conversation, mentioning Ingrid; or correcting a comment someone made about the dead child. Why was it the done thing to do to deny her when blind, and yet throw this almost inappropriate party when she is no longer disabled? "I'm surprised by this," Gregory says. "It's quite a gathering of people. The Jamesons didn't strike me as the kind of people for a big party."

"You'd be right there; Eilidh had nothing to do with this. I don't even think any of her family has turned up yet. No, this was Mark's idea." David nods towards the bar. "He's the landlord here. Managed to get in touch with the doctor who's been dealing with her rehabilitation. He's bringing her back to Shetland today. You heard much from Ingrid whilst she was away on the mainland?"

"I've not heard from her for months," Gregory says vaguely.

"I only heard about this yesterday," David continues. "News spreads quickly, doesn't it? Christ knows why everyone thought she was dead, but there's been some discussion and people thought it would be good to welcome her back to the islands; let her know she doesn't have to hide herself away anymore."

Gregory nods, as if in agreement, and takes a drink from his pint. He doesn't know what to say, other than despite well meant, there is something about all of this that feels rather inappropriate. Overwhelming. He is also jealous – he seems to be the last to know about her return, despite the fact that for the last few months he has been privy to her existence whereas most of the island's population thought her dead from childhood.

"It's a mind blower," David continues. "Not having seen a damn thing for two thirds of your life, and suddenly someone turns on the lights. You wouldn't know where to look first."

The inane chatter continues. Drink flows. A small buffet is set up at the side of the room. The hotel bar swells with people, most of whom are unfamiliar to Gregory. Everyone here seems to know everyone else, and he feels very much out of place, a tourist who has accidentally wandered into a private party and isn't quite sure how to sneak out. He sits at the side lines, a little dazed, more than apprehensive. The talk abruptly drops, word filters around that Ingrid and the doctor have arrived, and people look expectantly to the doorway. It feels as though they are waiting to toast the happy couple, the latest flame and object of local gossip.

A cheer rises through like a wave, people stand up from their tables to get a better view; Gregory half expects someone to rush forward and ask for an autograph. Through the gaps between arms and bodies, the viewpoint always moving, he sees her for the first time in three months, accompanied by a smartly dressed man with short cropped hair and wire-rimmed glasses – assumedly the doctor, for the way he leads her into the room by the elbow. Ingrid looks a little wan, overwhelmed, but trying to hide it. She smiles, but the expression doesn't reach her eyes. Her eyes. Now seeing. Now moving throughout the room, looking upon faces for the first time, soaking up an immense amount of information that has been closed off to her for so long. Despite everything – a brain tumour recently removed according to Shea – and rehabilitation, she looks well. Different. Her hair is tied up off her shoulders and back; she's a new person now. She is wearing a fitted sleeveless blue dress, the modern city girl. People shake her hand, greet her, smiling, clambering for her attention. The forced smile has gone as it is enough to simply try and keep up. Her eyes, her fresh gaze, wanders through the bar, scanning the faces, taking in all of these new people. She looks right at Gregory for a moment and he feels his chest tighten, but there is no reaction and she continues looking. Nothing more than a stranger, part of the background. And perhaps he is, now that she doesn't have to wait for company at the farm.

The excitement eventually levels, as it always must, and people get down to the serious business of socialising. The food is distributed; people take seats and start talking. There is pre-recorded music in the background, overfilled with happy banter and the clink of glasses. As it would happen, Ingrid and her doctor find their way to the next table up from Gregory and David. The doctor spreads his time between eagerly discussing his research – it seems Ingrid has been an excellent case study for him – and gazing tenderly and proudly at his protégée as if she is a prize winning pig. From the way he talks, she is still a long way from being completely rehabilitated and he intends to be with her for much longer. Probably forever if he can imagine it, judging from some of the possessive looks and body language. Ingrid's spatial awareness visually, as well as her hand-eye coordination were really weak when they first started working together, but they're making great progress. It's not something Gregory has considered, but he supposes there are all kinds of intricacies to learning to see again, things that most people do unconsciously. He watches as she picks up her glass, her focus solely on that glass. She wouldn't want to miss and knock it over, embarrass herself in front of all of these old and forgotten, and brand new friends. Someone has passed her a plate, a few sandwiches and sausage rolls, but she doesn't touch it. She looks at people when they speak to her, politely nods and vaguely smiles, but she seems tired and distracted.

At their table sit Gregory, David and a couple of local fishermen Gregory has already forgotten the names of. Although they have been conversing, it has been with half an ear, everyone paying more attention to the table next door.

"Ingrid," David takes advantage of a break in conversation, leaning across to put himself in her line of view. "I don't know if you'll remember me."

She looks at him and shakes her head.

"We have met; we went to the same school."

"Aye, but your voice'll've changed since then," someone says.

"Ever since his balls dropped." This sets off a chortle of amusement.

"I was friends with your brother," David continues. "David Henriksson."

"I can't remember..." This is the first time he has heard her speak. Her voice is quiet, the sentence falling away as if she's not sure what to say, or doesn't have the energy to finish the thought. It is another thing she must build her strength up for. She has an odd accent, a mix of the local Shetland, and some Edinburgh – an influence of the doctor in all probability. She speaks carefully, well pronounced as if speaking for a recording.

"Not to worry. It's grand to see you again," David reassures her.

"Well, lads," Anna-Mary joins the groups, standing behind the doctor, a gin and tonic in her hand. "Are you going to re-introduce me? I don't suppose Ingrid remembers me from school." She pauses, expecting someone to take up her case. "Well, come on. What about you, Gregory?"

There is a sudden rush of commotion as Ingrid lets out a little gasp as she knocks her drink over. In surprisingly little time a bar towel has appeared and is mopping up the spilt liquid. The doctor is reassuring Ingrid that this is just because of all the excitement, it's nothing to worry about and certainly won't set back her recovery. She doesn't appear to be listening, rather she is scanning the faces at the next table. The man closest to her is David Henriksson, whom she does remember as her brother's school friend but is not inclined to acknowledge; and three strangers. Or rather two strangers and one friend, but she cannot tell the three apart.

"Of course, you'll already know Gregory," David adds, "What with him staying at Lunna, you're neighbours. How long have you been staying on Shetland now?"

"Almost six months." Three words, four syllables, but already on the first, before it is fully pronounced, Ingrid's eyes have widened, and the first genuine smile has appeared. Because of course she recognises this voice, having listened to it for weeks long past, in pretence of not being able to hear. And there it is, she now knows who her friend is.

But the reunion is to be cut short, as Eilidh walks into the room, glancing around the party with a disapproving look. She quickly locates Ingrid, and does not appear to be happy, overjoyed, or any other emotion or any description to see that her daughter has regained her sight. Rather she looks keen to leave. "Ingrid," she speaks to her daughter, so naturally and without any awkwardness as though they have always talked, "I'm ready to take you home."

Ingrid looks from her mother to Gregory, regretfully, for she must leave already. She opens her mouth as if she is going to say something, speak to him directly for the first time, but the doctor is already full of activity, talking over her. "Yes, it's probably a good idea," he says, standing up from the table. "This is all a lot to take in. You don't want to overdo it."

As quickly as it happened, she is leaving again, getting up from the table and heading across to her mother. There is some fussing by the doors where the cases have been deposited. Ingrid leaves the hotel first, pulling her suitcase along with her. As the doctor moves to follow her, Eilidh steps in his way, her face taught. There is a low conversation between the two, of which Gregory cannot hear from this distance, but it ends in Eilidh leaving and the doctor staying, caught in limbo beside the exit. He clearly does not know what to do.

Eventually he slips into the crowds, setting himself on one of the bar stools, and slumps in front of his drink. And in that dejected move, it is clear that the Jamesons have decreed he is no longer of use.

Gregory does not stay in the Sumburgh Head Hotel particularly long. He doesn't find Anna-Mary again, although in fairness he doesn't look particularly hard. He walks back up to the bird station at the lighthouse to complete his paperwork. He leaves the lighthouse at six, and drives north to Lunna. The drive takes him almost an hour and a half. It has been a few weeks since he was last at the cottage for any kind of passing visit. As he drives down to the bay, passing the stone walls surrounding the little church yard, still water to his left, lime kilns on the edge of the land, he feels desolate. The light is fading fast, almost gone, the Lunna House Guesthouse like a grey ghost up on the hill. He turns off the road and parks up behind the guesthouse. He can not quite face going back to the Jameson's property yet, even though he will be a distance away from the main farmhouse, settled in his rudimentary cottage.

Miriam Rea, the landlady, looks surprised when he walks into the bar. Calum Moran is perched at the end of the bar, the fiddle left on the shelf for a week or so following an accident with a knife at work cutting salmon netting. "Gregory," she starts as he sits down on one of the vacant stools. She sounds a little uncertain. "We thought you'd be down at Sumburgh."

"Sumburgh?" Jesus, everyone but him knew about this gathering, this return to the islands.

"There was a wee welcome back for Ingrid."

"A wee welcome back from the dead," Calum mutters into his whisky.

"I've just come from there," Gregory admits. He nods to what Calum is drinking. "Can I get one of those?"

"That good, eh?"

"It's a strange carry on," Miriam agrees as she turns to get a measure of whisky in a glass. "Until two days ago we had no idea Ingrid was even alive. Everyone thought she'd died as a wee lassie. But then Jayne came in saying that she'd heard it from a friend in town that Ingrid Jameson had been on the mainland having an operation to get her eyesight fixed, and she was coming back to Shetland today. She'd need to get a lot more than her eyesight fixed, Jayne said, considering she's been dead heading on twenty years. But no, the woman was adamant, Ingrid's alive. She's just been living a bit of recluse on the family farm."

"It's the Jameson way," Calum adds darkly. "Keep it in the family."

"A recluse is one thing, but we're their closest neighbours. We had no idea. We've never even seen her. How can a person have been living just up the road all this time, and we've not caught so much as a glimpse?"

In a city it could be believed, but out here, this isolated, sparsely populated place, it truly fells like the impossible.

"You've been living on their property. Did you ever see her?"

"I got to know Ingrid before she went away."

"Gregory!" Miriam protests. "Why did you not think to tell us? How many times have you been in here?"

That question he can't answer, he's long lost track of how much time he'd spent at his sanctuary. He drinks the whisky. "No one ever said it was a secret but, it just felt like something you weren't supposed to talk about."

"That I can well believe," Calum says, setting his empty glass on the bar. "Can I get a top up?"

"I think I'll join you." Miriam takes a whisky bottle from under the bar, not hooked up for dispensing neat amounts, and pours for Calum and herself before topping up Gregory's without asking. It feels like it will be one of those evenings. "What kind of a neighbour do I feel like, having no idea the girl was alive. Stuck on that farm all these years. I'm surprised if she's not a headcase. Places like this, you need the community, your neighbours. You know, I have seen them now; I saw Eilidh drive past with a red-headed woman in the car. I assume it was Ingrid. I was surprised by how early they came by."

"She was barely in the hotel before Eilidh had turned up to take her away," Gregory says. "Ingrid's doctor had come over with her, but he was sent packing when Eilidh arrived."

"Was Shea there?"

The last words of Shea's on the subject had not been positive; he hadn't been surprised that she wasn't at the hotel. "She wasn't. None of the family was." Now that he thinks on it, this is a little surprising. On such an occasion, one would have expected the family to be present.

"Not even Andrew?"

"He lives in Edinburgh," Calum reminds Miriam. "He'll have been able to see her a lot these past couple of months."

"Aye, I suppose." Miriam runs a finger slowly around the rim of her glass, thinking over the revelations of the last couple of the days. "It's just not the done thing. What kind of an impression is this going to make on people like Gregory? That all islanders are like this?"

"I have already realised that the Jamesons aren't a typical case."

"People here care. We're a community, we help each other out."

"You're getting on your soap box," Calum warns.

"Well, I don't care." She is interrupted by the shrill call of the telephone. "Excuse me a moment, gentlemen."

Gregory doesn't leave until sometime after midnight. He has had a good number of whiskeys, and is suitably intoxicated, although he feels strangely sober. He leaves the car at the guesthouse – it would have to be incredibly bad luck to get caught drunk driving out here, but the last thing he needs is to drive it into a ditch and have to go cap in hand to the Jameson farm and ask John to pull his car out with one of the tractors.

The walk home is cold, although he does not feel it; only notices his steam breathe out in front of him. The cottage is still, damp, when he returns – it's been a while since it was properly lived in. He ought to have a fire going, but he is too sleepy to be bothered and too drunk to care. He kicks off his boots in the kitchen and goes fully dressed to his box bed.

Bright sunlight wakes him prematurely. He had neglected to shut the box bed doors and the intense clear light bites into his eyes.

Groaning, he rolls over and disappears into the bedding for another hour. When he eventually leaves his bed, noon is approaching, and he has a touch of a hangover in the background. He drinks a pint of cold water, gasping and squeezing his eyes shut for a moment. As if being refreshed in a glacier. Suddenly quite awake.

What to do now? In his car, back at the guesthouse, are his laptop and his notes. He could start work; there is enough to keep him occupied for weeks. He doesn't necessarily need to be here anymore. Part of him is keen to leave, if only to live on another part of Shetland. The other part is curious about the farmstead, about how things are now. But three months of no communication have been a long time, and he is uncertain of how welcome he is anymore.

Perhaps he will take a stroll around the farm, try to wake up; then track down John Jameson, and discuss cutting the tenancy short.

Putting on his boots, he leaves the cottage, heading up towards the hill. The sun still has some strength left in it at this time of year, and it feels good just to enjoy simple pleasures such as the heat of the sun on his face. Ahead walks a figure, heading in the direction of the cottage. It is Ingrid, and as soon as she realises he is out walking, she changes course slightly, coming for him. Gregory slows to a halt, stuffing his hands in his jacket pockets. He's not sure whether to be moody for the fact she never mentioned she was leaving for an operation; never mentioned when she was returning; or to be congratulatory on the fact that she's got her eyesight back. Or decided to start using her hearing again. He simply does not know how to behave with her.

She starts to talk – actually speak – but her voice is weak and tires easily, and cannot keep up with the flood of thoughts and information she needs to get out. She reverts to sign language, but he has grown rusty, and she is going too quickly for him to keep up. As she nears, the erratic embodiment comes into sharp focus; her hair is scruffily tied back as if she has just rushed out of the house with little attention to her appearance; her eyes are red-rimmed and puffy, and she seems nervous.

He can't follow what she is saying. Occasional words are picked up, others are misread, and his brain is translating nonsense. "Woah," he tells her, holding up his hands, already smiling. All thoughts of sulking and allegations gone. "I can't keep up with this."

She ignores him and continues with the fast sign language. He tries to concentrate, but can't follow; choking back on a laugh as he thinks he reads 'marry me' in the mix. This brings her up short and she abruptly ceases. "You're going to have to slow down or practice speaking, because I'm misreading all of this. I'm sure you're not saying half the things I think you are."

"*Marry me.*"

He feels like he has swallowed a stone. His stomach is trying to digest it. He must have mislearned that word.

"*M-A-R-R-Y M-E.*"

Oh Jesus Christ. Perhaps he is still drunk, or this is just a strange dream, and he will wake up in his box bed with a stomping headache. He runs his hands over his face. He is definitely here. When he dares to look back out from the confines of his immediate space, Ingrid is right in front of him. She clutches on to his hands as if she is pleading for her life. To put gravity behind the request, she uses her fragile vocal chords on the case. "Marry me."

"Ingrid," he groans, despite himself allowing his fingers to curl around her hands, just in case she might change her mind and dart away. And certainly it is a temptation; who would want to turn down a pretty young woman who appears to be throwing herself at him. It's not like Gregory's ever had a proposal before. He's not been the overly romantic type, and he simply doesn't have the looks to make women swoon. But this isn't right. "What's going on?"

She is forced to speak because she doesn't have the use of her hands, tugging for him to follow. "Come to the farm."

He follows because... because he cannot help himself. There is not much conversation, for Ingrid can't manage long discussions yet, she is distracted and Gregory is not sure whether he wants the answers to his questions. It is a surprise to find both Eilidh and John in the farm yard together. They are talking, Eilidh wiping her hands on her apron, the sheepdog skulking around her ankles. They look up at the sound of footsteps.

"Ingrid," John starts, sounding as though he is surprised to see her.

"I have news," she speaks, still holding onto Gregory's hand. He is surprised to feel her trembling.

Eilidh folds her arms. John barely raises his eyebrows. It is like a standoff.

"We're getting married."

The reaction doesn't include the usual screams of delight at the mention of wedding bells. Eilidh purses her lips and narrows her eyes, but doesn't look to be particularly surprised. Of all of them, Gregory included, John seems to be the most dislocated, as if having stumbled home after years lost at sea. "Married?" He looks from Ingrid to Gregory. "And how long has this been going on?"

Ingrid starts to say something, but Eilidh interrupts her. "Is this true?"

This is the moment. The chance to say it's not true, I never said yes. Your daughter is crazy and I wash my hands of all of you. Turn and walk away. Get the car and drive away from here forever. But the truth is not forth coming. He can't throw her back into all of this, and besides which, he is more than flattered, if he can just continue ignoring the rational voice pointing out that flattery isn't a good enough reason to screw up the rest of your life.

Eilidh is waiting for a denial which will not come.

"I didn't think I'd see this day," John breaks the awkward silence. "I suppose congratulations are in order." He looks at Gregory. "You'd better look after her."

Eilidh turns and goes back into the farmhouse. John shuffles awkwardly, the atmosphere particularly icy. In anyone else this would look like extreme disappointment in the choice of future spouse, but normal rules of behaviour don't seem to apply to Eilidh. "I'd better get back to work," John says apologetically. And with that, the deed is done. Gregory is no longer a bachelor.

The day flies by, surreal, and once started, it is difficult to rein it in. Ingrid goes to her flat and comes out directly with a small suitcase and canvas bag full of books – already packed in advance – and announces that she is going to live with Gregory. In the cottage. In the cold. Where there is no hot water. If they are going ahead with this, the least they could do is move into her comfortable flat. But she is adamant about making a fresh break. This is going to be a change in her life.

They walk back to the cottage together, Gregory carrying the suitcase, barely saying anything. He is still giddy as new things occur to him with every minute. Just exactly what all of this is going to entail. They get back to the cottage, to a damp, cold hole. He has still not lit that fire.

"I'm thinking of leaving here, moving to somewhere a bit more modern for the winter."

Ingrid enters the room and sits down at the kitchen table. She suddenly looks immensely tired, barely capable of hearing him.

"We can go to Lerwick tomorrow," she says in her quiet way, as though this is a relaxation of the original plan. "To give notice."

"Notice of what?"

"Marriage."

"Tomorrow?" Gregory coughs. "Come on, what's going on here? I've not heard from you for three months, then you reappear and want to get married. Get married tomorrow..."

"Give notice."

"Ok, give notice then."

"It takes fifteen days. We can be married in a month."

A month of freedom left. He is a little surprised that he hasn't already thrown her out of the cottage. Perhaps that operation on her brain had a few other side effects besides restoring her sight. But there is the guilty reasoning as well. Obviously something must be wrong, normal people don't do this. But he can also take advantage of the situation, tie Ingrid to him. Under normal circumstances would he really have a fair chance of catching a woman like Ingrid?

"Are you going to tell me what's going on?"

She looks up at him. "Do you have your birth certificate?"

"Not with me."

"How soon?"

"How soon can I get it? I have no idea. My mother's probably got a copy; I could ask her to post it."

Ingrid seems to be satisfied with this answer. She smiles weakly, yawns and rubs her eyes – eyes now with pupils, eyes that can see him. Enough has been discussed for one day. Things are not completely resolved, but there is a plan in place and little more to do for today. "I need to sleep. I didn't sleep last night." She rises from the table and pads through to the bedroom, already mistress of the cottage. Sitting on the edge of the box bed, she unties her laces, and leaves her shoes on the floor as she hooks her legs up to fold herself into the bed.

Gregory feels as though he has been dismissed. "I've got to go fetch the car," he calls through to her, before once again leaving the cottage. The breeze outside slaps him square on the face. What the hell do you think you're doing?

He walks down the road, back to Lunna, in something of a daze, and is grateful for the fact that he does not bump into anyone. Not that they could possibly know about Ingrid's engagement – it's taken almost twenty years to learn she's not actually dead – but he feels as though it is written upon his face. There's no denying it.

When he returns to the croft, John Jameson is waiting outside, slouched against the cottage wall. He nods to the front door as Gregory turns off the engine and opens the car door. "Ingrid's asleep inside."

"Do you want me to tell her...?"

"No," he shakes his head, wistfully staring at the ground. Earth his family have farmed upon for generations. The end of the line, for none of his offspring have shown any interest in continuing the good work. "It was you I wanted a word with."

Is this to be the threatening father of the bride talk: if you ever hurt my little princess, I'll hunt you down and break every bone in your body. Instead John takes a crumpled brown envelope from his back pocket and passes it to Gregory. "This is for Ingrid; for the wedding," he explains. "Don't... don't tell her I gave you this. Pretend it's yours or whatever. She wouldn't take it from me. Got her own money. Independent woman."

Gregory takes the envelope. In his own way, his own man-of-few-words way, John is trying, has tried, but the Jameson family as a unit was never quite to be. "I've been toying with the idea of moving. For the winter. I know we agreed the lease for a year..."

"Don't worry about that. It'll be cold in there over winter." He gives the cottage one last look. "Got to get back to the farm," he tells Gregory, before heading back away to the fields.

Inside Ingrid is in a deep sleep. She is on her side, facing the box bed doors. Her hair falls over her face in a tangle, revealing a section of scalp with short stubby hair – a band that must have been shaved down for the operation. Brain surgery is a very serious procedure, he thinks as he crouches down in front of her. There are a lot of risks involved. In fact, it must have been quite frightening going into hospital for the operation. She has had an eventful year, a distinct change from the way she usually spends her time. Her sight has been restored, and perhaps anything seems possible. She is ready for a change, a fresh start. To get married. But why even come back here, if she is so keen to get away? Surely that young doctor would have leapt at the chance if she'd asked him to marry her. Gregory flatters himself with the notion that she came back for him, although he knows deep down that things are not that simple.

Later that night, the first night of this new, odd platonic romance, they are together in the box bed. Ingrid is asleep, but Gregory is unable to lose consciousness, too aware of her presence, the change in the air. The enclosure of the box bed means that her scent is almost intoxicating. At one point she is dreaming, mumbling, distressed. He can't understand, she has reverted to another language unknown to him. Scottish Gaelic or Irish Gaelic, he's not sure, in fact he'd forgotten completely about the connection until now. He recalls his first visit to the Jameson property, Eilidh emerging from the farmhouse and scolding her son, as soon as she is sure Gregory does not understand.

Abruptly Ingrid rolls over, still unconscious, and clutches him as if she may be swept away otherwise. It takes him by surprise, but he puts an arm around her back, as if to stop the bad dreams. And he knows this is all wrong, marriage in a month, engagement without declarations of undying love, but the longer this goes on, the less chance there is he will put a stop to things.

His mother is screaming with joy down the telephone. Gregory feels like a fraud. He grimaces, holding the mobile phone away from his ear for a moment. Surely they are both too old for this kind of reaction.

"Oh, Gregory, I never thought I'd see the day."

Perhaps not the most positive of statements, but it is not meant unkindly. He is sat on a low car park wall along the sea front in Lerwick, his back to the waters, facing the shops and a turn in to Commercial Street. He is waiting for Ingrid. Since making the step to leave the family home, her confidence and independence are growing. She wanted to do something – wouldn't say what – in town on her own and arranged to meet Gregory at the car park later. Perhaps in a month's time she won't need him, and the idea of marriage will be discarded, the ever hopeful Gregory left standing at the altar.

"Is this the girl you were living with?"

"No." Why would she ask about Jennifer? That had been over years ago. "It's someone I've met here, on Shetland."

"And you're getting married already?"

"It's not a big deal."

"Not a big deal! That hardly sounds like love's young dream."

"I mean we're not making a big thing of it; no big ceremony. It'll just be at the registrar's office."

"In Edinburgh?"

"No, here in Lerwick. It will be in the next month or so." They haven't booked a date yet, but as neither of them have nine to five jobs at the moment, it will be easy to fit in with the registrar's schedule. They have already been to the registrar to give notice. Gregory doesn't have his birth certificate here, but the registrar is happy to proceed on the understanding that he will be able to check the document in the next week or so.

"So soon? Your brother's not going to be able to come over for that..."

"We don't need anyone..."

"I intend to be there, my boy," his mother cuts him short. "You make sure you let me know the date as soon as it's fixed. And I'll get my passage sorted out. Now, are you going to tell me something about this girl? What's she called?"

"Ingrid."

"Ingrid? Is she Scandinavian then?"

"No, she's a local. She lives near to where I've been staying."

"And what does she do?"

What does Ingrid do? She's never had a job or a profession in the traditional sense. She studies, she writers articles for various publications. And up until recently, she hid away on the farm, avoiding the world. "She writes," he eventually answers. "Articles for magazines. That kind of thing."

"Very good. Pretty lass, is she?"

He looks up, just as Ingrid emerges on to the road further up. The sun is at its height in the day, the light shining off the red-gold in her hair. Pretty isn't the word, he thinks. She is captivating. He feels his chest tighten; anticipation ball up in his stomach. This woman is with him. He can ignore the finer details, the cracks in that image. "Yes. Yes she is."

"I can't wait to meet her. I've got to go now, but you make sure you keep me updated."

"I will. Don't forget to post my birth certificate."

"I won't. Goodbye."

Ingrid has a new rucksack slung over one shoulder. As she reaches Gregory, she sits beside him on the wall, slipping the rucksack to the ground between her feet. It looks full, reasonably well packed. She's obviously had a successful expedition.

"Get everything you wanted?"

"Yes. I'm finished here." She shrugs into her jacket as the wind blows in off the sea. Leans into him, for a windbreak.

"What do you want to do now?"

"We could go look at the cottage?" There is a short term lease at very reasonable rates over the winter period, just outside of Lerwick. It is a modest building, not many rooms and simple furniture, but compared to the crofter's cottage at Lunna, it looks like a palace from the pictures they have seen on the internet. The thought of hot running water and decent electrics sound like heaven.

"Might as well."

She moves to get up, but Gregory lingers on the wall. Since visiting the registrar, filling in the forms and saying those words out loud to his mother, the enormity of what he has agreed to do, what they will be doing in a month's time, has really hit him. This is supposed to be a lifetime commitment. Is it right to jump from a few months' of friendship to a knee-jerk reaction marriage in under a year of knowing one another? As much as he is thrilled by the idea of having a wife like Ingrid, there is that niggling doubt of her own motivations. That and somehow they are selling themselves short, missing out on so much more. If she's still sure, he wants to try and do this properly. "You've not changed your mind; no second thoughts?"

"No." She is quite adamant in her response.

"Can I ask why?"

"Why?"

"Why you want to marry me?" Perhaps he is pushing his luck, or requesting an answer he doesn't really want to hear. But he needs to be clear in his own mind.

She looks a little surprised that he might ask such a thing. Bites the side of her lip thoughtfully. She is not thinking of an answer, because she already knows that part; only how to phrase it, how much to give away. "You are the kindest person I ever met."

"Kindest?" he can't help the slight laugh of surprise that escapes him.

"To me," she adds. She lowers her eyes. "When you met me, I was in..." She stops, unable or unwilling to continue. She can feel her eyes welling up, but will not cry, for these dark reasons are not worth her tears.

"Ok, I'm not trying to make you upset." He puts a reassuring arm around her shoulders, pulling her across to him. It is all very platonic. That will take a little longer he supposes. "If we're going to do this, I want to do it properly. Other people have it properly, so I don't see why you should be any different. Not just some rushed lip service..."

"I want to do this soon."

"I know. That's not exactly what I meant. I have something for you." He had his own things to do whilst she disappeared into the small shopping area of Lerwick. He is not particularly good at selecting jewellery for women; girlfriends in the past had always been a little disappointed by his lack of understanding of their personal style, but he doesn't want to think that Ingrid is going to miss out on all the little rituals that make up a life, simply because she is so keen to get married and get away. The woman in the shop, a kindly soul who immediately took to mothering him when she realised just how uncertain and inept he was, had taken a larger input into which ring to pick than he had, but this is the best he can come up with on short notice. He had taken the ring out of the box whilst he was speaking to his mother on the phone, looking at the stone settings and design before slipping it loose back into his pocket. He takes the ring out again now. "I don't know if this is your kind of thing..."

"Oh no, you don't have to do this." Ingrid looks guilty. Positively undeserving.

"Yes I do. Everyone else gets this. Why shouldn't you?"

"Because..."

He takes her left hand and slips the ring on her finger. "Lucky fit."

Ingrid darts forward to hug him. "Thank you," she says quietly, certain now that she has made the right choice. With her arms around Gregory's neck, she holds out her left hand to take a proper look at the ring. She's not sure she has any particular taste in these things yet, but the sentiment is that which is important, and besides, it already looks quite pleasing to her eye. As he had said, lucky fit.

They move into the new cottage two weeks before the wedding. The property was vacant, and having looked around it, Gregory is unable to resist the creature comforts for long. Although Ingrid doesn't push for the move, he senses she is relieved to get away from the Jameson farm.

The cottage is just off the main road outside the village Hamnavoe. In a plot of green grass on a slight rise, the house looks boldly out onto the bay, double glazed windows proof against the wind from the Atlantic. On the west side of Shetland, just below Scalloway, the village sits at the top of an island called West Burra, connected to the mainland by a bridge. With about an hour's driving between Lunna and Hamnavoe, Ingrid feels as though she has finally moved away. Edinburgh was much further of course, but a hospital is never a preferable home.

A few days in to the new venture, and Ingrid is moving in properly, unknown to Gregory. He has been out walking in the morning on the headland north of the cottage, past fields, a small farm and out onto moorland. At the very top, away from the reach of roads, the sparse tourist trail and general attention, he is pleased to find a small white sandy bay. Had it still been the summer, this would have been perfect. Ingrid does not join him that morning, making some reference to not feeling too well and staying in bed. He has no reason to think she would have anything else planned, concealed by tales of headaches, and strikes out on his own.

He arrives back at the cottage earlier than probably either of them would suppose. Eilidh's car is parked up by the cottage behind his own car. Ingrid is outside, and mother and daughter are talking, a mixture of speech and sign language, as if Ingrid can't quite let go of the old ways. They don't see him approaching the house across the land from the north. He knows he ought to make his presence known, but he cannot help himself, and instead stops at the side of the cottage, to watch and listen, unseen.

"That's everything you asked for," Eilidh is saying. "When you get settled somewhere more permanent, let me know where you want the rest of it sending." She puts her hands on her hips and surveys the modern little cottage. "You'll have a more comfortable winter in here, no doubt. You going to tell me what the grand master plan behind all this is?"

"*I just want to try being happy.*"

"And you think this will do it?"

"*The last plan didn't work.*"

"Well, I did warn you, you'd find no peace," Eilidh says rather solemnly. "The best thing you can do now is get away, start again."

Ingrid simply nods and looks at the ground. She is a mirror of her mother, both women solitary creatures alone in their own spheres. It seems that both want to do, say more, but are restrained and will never take the final step.

"I hear you're getting married in a couple of weeks. Let it be a fresh start." Eilidh puts her hands into the pockets of her green jacket. She looks up at the sky, like a fisherwoman checking the weather before setting off in her boat. "I've got to get going."

And with that, Eilidh gets into her car and reverses down the short drive back to the road. She is gone and Ingrid is left quite alone. She stands motionless for a few moments, her hair blowing in the breeze. She brushes it behind her ear, turns, and goes back indoors.

Gregory backs away from the cottage, goes around a field to get down onto the road. He then walks home, coming up the drive and through the front door. There are four cardboard boxes stacked in the living room. Ingrid is perched on the arm of the settee, poking through the contents of one of the boxes. She looks up as Gregory walks in.

"What's all this?" He is the perfect actor. Perhaps she is too, he reflects, as she folds the lid back down on the box. There is so much of her earlier life that he knows nothing about.

"My things," she answers. She needs to keep practising talking, and Gregory is purposefully ignoring the sign language to get her to exercise her vocal chords. "My mother came by earlier."

"Oh, I hadn't realised she was coming." Since Ingrid moved in with him, he has not seen any of her family.

"It wasn't planned."

He's not entirely convinced, but doesn't pull her up on it. "Do you still want to go over to Lerwick this afternoon?"

"Yes, if it's still ok."

"Give me half an hour. I've just got a couple of emails to reply to."

They go to Lerwick to do the food shop. Ingrid is oddly quiet, even by her standards, and Gregory finds the car radio is his biggest source of company on the journey across the island. On the way back towards Hamnavoe, Ingrid leans her head against the passenger window, her eyes lazily moving from the view of the inlet up the side of Scalloway, to the road ahead. She looks over to Gregory as they drive over the first bridge onto East Burra, heading onwards to the next bridge that will take them to their own island. "Is it difficult?"

"Difficult?" He glances over at her. "Is what difficult?"

"Driving?"

"Driving?" He is surprised by this question. For a foolish moment he wonders that she has got to the age she has and never driven a car, but of course she hasn't, driving is a freedom the blind have to forego. "Once you get used to it, it's just second nature. It's not much of a problem here; there's so little traffic."

"I never tried it." She sinks back into the seat and laughs a little to herself. "Not surprising. I couldn't see until a few months ago."

"It was probably the sensible thing to do."

"Do you think I'd be able to learn?"

"Why not?"

After he's driven over the second bridge, now onto West Burra, he pulls off onto the junction of a small road to the left, where a couple of industrial buildings are. It's the middle of the afternoon; they've not seen any traffic. He puts the vehicle into neutral, leaves the engine idling. "Do you want to try?"

"Now?" Ingrid looks horrified.

"Why not?"

She pauses, and it looks like she will turn down the offer, but changes her mind at the last moment. "It's not far back home now, all right."

Gregory turns off the engine, and they swap places in the car. Ingrid readjusts the seat so that her feet reach the peddles, she grips the steering wheel, in the classic position of a learner, leaning forward, and looks across at him. "Ok. Tell me the basics."

"Ok, very important," he starts, tapping the handbrake between them. "This is the handbrake. When this is on, the car will not go anywhere. So it's really important you take that off before you drive off. It can bugger up the car otherwise. You push the button on the top in, and then let the lever go down.

"The three foot pedals in the footwell are the clutch, break and accelerator. You use your left foot on the clutch, right foot either on the break or the accelerator. You're either wanting to go faster or slower, but not both at the same time, so you only use one at a time."

"And the clutch?"

"You only press the clutch down when you're wanting to change gear. You've got first through to fifth depending on how fast you're going, then reverse to go back."

"How do you know when to change?"

"It's the revs of the engine; you'll hear it when you need to go up a gear. Just press the clutch to the floor now. So put the gear stick into first."

Ingrid puts her hand on top of the gear stick, a little uncertain. "Just straight up?"

"To the side." Gregory puts his hand on top of hers, moving the gear stick. "So that's up into first. When you're just setting off. Then down to second, back up in the middle for third, down for fourth, and then up to fifth. You only get up into that on the main road here; you need to be doing over forty miles an hour." His hand lingers over hers as the gear stick is moved back into neutral. They've touched hands so many times in the past, it being their only way to talk. Now that the spoken word is taking precedent, hands are taking on another use. This feels like the closest physical touch he's had with her since she's come back from Edinburgh. Only two weeks before the wedding.

"Ok," Ingrid unknowingly breaks his train of thought as she pulls on her seat belt. "Let's give it a go."

"You sure?"

"It's not far. I should try new things." She twists the key in the ignition and the engine sparks back to life. She's been in the car many times, but suddenly the engine seems more powerful, almost overwhelming as she is sat in control.

"Right, put your foot on the clutch, and get it into first."

This is the easy bit.

"It's pretty flat, so you can take the handbrake off now."

Done.

"To drive off, you need to gently raise your foot off the clutch as you give it some gas, you know, use the accelerator..."

The engine roars as Ingrid gives the car a bit too much gas. "Jesus, this isn't as easy as it looks." She clutches the steering wheel like an old lady, looks across at him and grins. "OK, I can do this." The engine revs more gently, and the car makes movement of rolling forward. She gets too confident and lets her foot jump off the clutch. There is a heavy thud sound and the car jerks forward before stopping, the engine silent.

"You've stalled the car."

"And that's bad?"

Gregory shrugs. "Well, we're not going to get anywhere, but you wouldn't be a learner driver if you don't do the bunny hops. Put it back in neutral; twist the key back round to turn off the ignition and then start again."

Ingrid gets the car engine running again, and puts it into first. "I am going to do this," she mutters, more to herself than to reassure Gregory. Leaning forward, as if trying to will the car on with her mental focus, she presses down on the accelerator and eases off the clutch. It's not a brilliant start, the car juddering and shaking. "I'm going to stall again."

"No you're not; give it a bit more gas." Gregory looks over his shoulder, checking there isn't any traffic coming up behind them. The car starts to move forward, Ingrid gasping in delight as she has now properly driven her first metre. The car seems to be heading towards the building. "Just remember about the steering." Gregory pushes on the steering wheel, getting the car back onto the road as the engine bites properly, happily in first and driving.

"I'm driving!" Ingrid looks delighted, as if she has performed a miracle. The revs roar louder as the speed approaches ten miles an hour.

"You want to go up into second now."

"Second?"

"Same as before. Put your foot right down on the clutch; bring the gear stick down into second, then gently up."

They drive along the road like a pair of pensioners; juddering along at around fifteen miles an hour, but Ingrid is ecstatic that she is actually driving, second gear, along a road. "Our turn off is coming up."

"Indicator's here. Just flick it up to turn right." It doesn't matter, there's no one else on the road, but he ought to do this properly.

"Do you think I need to slow down?"

"I think you'll manage the corner at the speed we're going."

She turns the wheel, the car going down the side road.

"You'll maybe want to get into first; it's a tight corner onto our drive. You'll have to give it a bit of welly to get up the hill."

Ingrid bunny hops around the corner, Gregory thankful there are no imposing stone gateposts to drive through; and revs the car up the short drive, pulling sharply on the wheel to bring the car around the back of the cottage and abruptly slamming on the break, neglecting to put her foot on the clutch at the same time and stalling the car again. They both lurch forward, and Gregory puts the handbrake on. Not the most thorough of lessons, he thinks, but it had been a very impromptu introduction to driving.

Ingrid lurches forward with the final stall behind the cottage; still thrilled by the fact she has driven a car; and then strains against her seat belt, leaning across the front of the car to thrown her arms around him in victory. Her face is very close to his, and perhaps for the first time she is able to look at him close up, the fine details of his face and his expression. Gregory feels her loose hair brush against the side of his face. She is so very close that he is physically aware of the breath moving in and out of her body. She opens her mouth, thinking to say something more, but the words aren't forthcoming, and she looks him in the eye. He feels an almost overwhelming desire to possess her physically at that moment. Two weeks before marriage and they have not so much as even kissed.

"I..." Ingrid starts, her voice very light. She lowers her eyelids slightly, as if shyly, and moves up closer against him. She places her mouth to his, and yet not, a breath at most between their lips, just leaving an anticipation teasingly hanging in the space. Gregory crosses over the void, kissing her for the first time, her hands on the side of his face. With this release, everything comes flooding, fast, suddenly, intensely. He unsnaps the seatbelt, as Ingrid shrugs herself out of her own belt, to then clamber over the gear stick to straddle his lap. It is a confined space in the front of the car, Ingrid hunched over, almost sitting on the dashboard. He allows his hands the freedom to move, up the side of her torso to the form of her breasts through her sweater. Ingrid works surprisingly quickly. Already she has unbuttoned his shirt and unfastened his belt. There is a desperation, as if she has been waiting for him to do this for months. She pulls her top and sweater up and over her head in one go, her skirt having ridden up to her hips already. In what feels like seconds, she is all but naked, aside from the skirt around her waist and the shoes on her feet, her breasts pressed up against his chest, her body sinking down onto him as he feels himself harden, Ingrid guiding him up inside her.

And so that awkward doubt that this might only ever be platonic is erased. The future husband and wife make love for the first time in cramped conditions in the front of their car, the windows steaming up in a typically clichéd way, and Gregory now quite convinced that there is nothing what so ever to worry about.

They are married on a Tuesday. The ceremony is held in the registry office in central Lerwick, a few streets back from the main shopping street. The registry office sits within a small complex of official buildings, next door to the police station. It almost looks like a residential building, with grey stone granite walls, blue grey slate roof tiles and an unprepossessing facade all to reflect the dismal winter that approaches. There is a strip of ornate ironwork running across the peak of the main roof, as if to denote this building has a special purpose, and that is all.

Ingrid arrives in a long sleeved cream dress – not a wedding dress per say, just a dress that happens to be a traditional bridal colour. Nothing about this day is to be a grand statement, an over indulgence. It is a stark contrast to the average twenty thousand pounds – or whatever the latest figure is – a British wedding 'ought' to cost, according to magazines. In some respects this is better, it cripples no one financially, and does not set up any false expectations or an overwhelming anti climax for the day after. As much as every marriage is special, for most people it is not a national event and countrywide occasion for celebration. In opposition, Ingrid has been so casual and unconcerned, whilst at the same time keen to see it completed, that Gregory is surprised it is he who has forced the more romantic, superfluous touches onto the day. The flowers she carries – Ingrid walks down the aisle on her own – were his idea, as were the rings. As is the lunch at one of the hotels overlooking the sea.

Not one of the Jameson family is present for the wedding. Ingrid is unconcerned, although Gregory's mother, who has made the trip all the way from Beverley in North Yorkshire, asks what has happened; why the local girl has no one at the ceremony. Alan Brun, Gregory's old university friend now living on Fair Isle, serves as a witness, as does Alan's current girlfriend, Libby, for Ingrid. The ceremony goes frighteningly quickly. It is surreal in how easy and quick it is, just a signature in a book at the end, and then they are bound in a legal agreement that will be complicated and expensive to get out of should they ever change their minds. The deed is done, Gregory is now a married man – the last thing he would have expected when planning his year out at Shetland – and Ingrid is no longer a Jameson, having decided probably even before she asked Gregory to marry her, that she would be changing her name to Hughson.

Gregory's mother sits in the front row and cries with joy that her eldest has finally married. Her younger son, now living in Canada, married over ten years ago, has three children; whilst Gregory seemed to wander in the wilderness alone. Not that he suffered for it, Gregory had always been quite content with his own company, but she is the kind of woman who likes to see everyone coupled off.

Alan takes photographs for them, both inside the registrar's office, and outside, where although chilly, the sun is shining unobstructed. Whilst standing for yet another photo, Gregory notices Eilidh across the road near the Island Council building. Her arms are folded and she stands in something of a satisfied stance. He starts to raise his hand, as if to wave her over, but she simply shakes her head. All of the Jamesons knew the time and the date of the marriage, he had made certain of that, but none had been particularly keen in coming. Shea, whom he had bumped into in Lerwick, had been particularly livid, although even today he cannot work out exactly why.

From the registrar's office, the small party take a couple of taxis to the hotel where they are joined by the few people Gregory has gotten to know on Shetland since he moved here – the locals at Lunna: Miriam and husband who own the guesthouse, Calum, Jayne and Hugo Castleton; none of whom are surprised to find that not one of Ingrid's relations have shown their face. The only person to query it is his mother, but as she realises every other person present accepts this as the way Ingrid's family are, she stops asking and decides to mother Ingrid instead, who in turn finds all this attention very unfamiliar. Gregory had also asked Anna-Mary; as the manager of the phalarope programme he had worked on, he felt out of form he ought to, but he is relieved when she rather tersely informs him she already has other plans for that day.

The lunch time celebrations continue into the early evening; although the party is small, Gregory has managed to gather together a number of Shetlanders who enjoy to talk, and coupled with his mother's curiosity about life up here (she has never been further north than Edinburgh), they probably could have talked through the entire weekend had the hotel not needed the room for a seven o'clock dinner booking.

Gregory's mother flies back to Edinburgh to get a train to Yorkshire the following day. Gregory and Ingrid stay on Shetland through the winter. Gregory completes his work on the upcoming tourist book, including all revisions requested by the publisher; and also works on a couple of papers for periodicals. Ingrid practices her driving along the single lane back roads around the cottage with him, and continues with her rehabilitation. There are vocal exercises to complete to strengthen her voice after years of inactivity; and she must learn to read again. Although she still prefers Braille, she accepts that there is so much more available to her as written literature, and it is something she must train herself to do. She spends many afternoons in the living room by the window overlooking the grey and frequently foggy winter bay, reading books from the library. Unconsciously her fingers will move over the pages, as if half-expecting to find another story embossed within the paper.

They spend Christmas on the island in the cottage. There is no need for extended family visits. Gregory's mother is in Canada over the festive period, and Gregory can't imagine that the Jameson farmhouse will be full of yuletide joy. He doesn't ask Ingrid about it, and she mentions no desire to go back.

Spring emerges back home, but so far north, it is always late on Shetland. They leave the islands just as spring is starting, Gregory now having completed his year on the islands. It is time to return to Edinburgh, his tenants for the year having moved out just after Christmas, leaving his home waiting for reoccupation. Ingrid is quite happy to leave the islands, showing no particular regret or longing when he brings up the subject. Gregory sells that car that has transported him without problem the past year, they give up the cottage, pack their belongings, sending a certain amount ahead of them. Boarding the ferry in the afternoon to travel back to Aberdeen overnight, Gregory feels a pang of sadness. It's been a strange year, not always what expected and not everyone has been what one might describe as welcoming, but there is a spirit and a camaraderie he will miss. He has become accustomed to the treeless landscape of Shetland, the ragged, rugged coastline, the people, the rich greenness, and the incredible peace. He will be sorry to leave. But he is coming home with a lot more than he would have expected this time last year.

Home is a small terrace house in Duddingston, an area of Edinburgh around the back of Holyrood Park, between Arthur's Seat and Portobello by the sea. He cannot see the rugged uplands of Holyrood park from his house or garden – it's positioned too far down the slope and around the curve of the road for that, but it is only a short walk through the housing area before he can be in Holyrood, striding through the rough grass, past gorse bushes, and half-fooling himself that he is in the Highlands.

It takes some time to get used to being in Edinburgh, perhaps more so for Gregory than Ingrid, who had spent three summer months in the city regaining her sight and experiencing having this extra sense. Suddenly there are trees, streets and lines of houses that go on forever, traffic at all times of the night, and a sky that never goes completely pitch black. There is no sea air, no thick drifting landscapes of fog and no complete solitude. He is surprised just how much he misses Shetland. Ingrid will not admit that she misses her home country, but there are moments when she seems overwhelmed by the immensity of the city.

Gregory gets some work from the university marking exam papers at the beginning of summer, to earn some money before he returns to full time teaching at the autumn. Ingrid, who has never had a real job in the usual understanding of the word, manages to find employment surprisingly easily, going onto a contract with the council for teaching special needs children. She takes on one recently blinded child who needs to learn how to read Braille; and another older child who is deaf-blind and struggling with secondary school studies due to a lack of knowledgeable teachers who can communicate with the deaf-blind sign language. To have someone who is fluent and has had many years reliant on these systems is something of a Godsend.

At the end of May exams start, and Gregory heads over to the Geography department one afternoon to pick up papers for marking. It's a glorious day, and he walks through Holyrood Park to get there – his main base of employment unfortunately located pretty much the opposite side of Holyrood Park to his home, which means there is no quick direct route. On days like this, it doesn't seem to matter. He is just turning off The Pleasance to go up Drummond Street to the Geography department when he sees Andrew Jameson walking down the other side of the street to him.

"Andrew."

Andrew slows, having heard his name and been awakened from his thoughts. He glances over his shoulder, back up the road, before scanning in front of him and catching sight of Gregory. He nods a hello.

"How are things with you?" Gregory crosses over cobbled street, a group of first year university girls trotting past him, chattering about how stressed they are, clutching files and rolling their eyes.

"Not too bad. So you're back in civilisation, eh? Been a while. I was beginning to think you'd got stranded over there."

"Almost. We've been back about a month now. Still not completely used to all this. It's funny how much I miss the place."

"Aye? Well, no accounting for taste."

"Listen, you should come over sometime. Catch up with Ingrid."

"Ingrid?" Andrew seems to stiffen a little, taking an unconscious step back. "What's she doing in Edinburgh?"

Gregory feels his genuine smile falter a little. "I thought Eilidh said she would tell..."

"My mother? I am not in regular contact with my family. I thought you would have picked up on that when we went up there." Andrew looks mildly irritated. "I've heard some random stories about Ingrid getting her eyes sorted..."

"She was here in Edinburgh, three months last summer. I thought you would have seen her."

"I didn't know. Mind you, that's not the weirdest story I did hear. Apparently she got..." he stops, looking at Gregory again. "You said we."

"Sorry?"

"You said 'we've been back about a month'. Oh Jesus, you're not telling me it's true, are you? My sister did get married. It wasn't you, was it? Did you marry Ingrid?"

Gregory is taken aback by this response. Andrew has always seemed so laid back, happy-go-lucky. Moving in with a woman within a week of meeting has happened on more than one occasion with Andrew. Gregory does not expect him to be judgemental. Besides, for a family that is self-confessed disinterested in one another, it seems strange to be emotional. "She could have done worse."

"Shit, man, I don't mean..." Andrew's shoulders slump, his eyes drifting to the end of the road, where it joins The Pleasance. "She couldn't have done any better. It's just a shock. I'm out of touch with what goes on up there. Congratulations."

It doesn't sound convincingly sincere, but Gregory doesn't push the issue. Perhaps this has reminded Andrew just how estranged from his own family he really is. The rebelling and the good times in Edinburgh might have been great for him, but he never thought they'd cut him off as well as him doing just that to them. "You should come over sometime," Gregory repeats the offer. "It would be good. Ingrid doesn't know many people here yet."

"Yeah." Andrew's attention has wandered back to the end of the road, watching the cars drive up the Pleasance. "Sometime. I've got to go now. I'm going to be late for a meeting with my supervisor."

Andrew sets off along the road, leaving Gregory on the pavement feeling as though he's put two left feet in an awkward situation, although not quite sure how. He wonders about asking Ingrid. She doesn't talk about her family, but then again he's never asked. He wonders why the Jamesons are the way they are. When he gets home later that day, she seems distracted and unwilling to talk. She is at the kitchen table, her files out and paperwork half filled in. She is tapping her pen on the corner of a form, where a blotchy ink mark is forming. She continues on form whilst Gregory potters in the kitchen, making noise and starting to prepare the evening meal, before she mutters something about a headache and going upstairs for a rest.

He goes up to the bedroom when the food is ready, to find out if she wants anything. She is awake but uncommunicative, lying on her side on the bed, staring vacantly out of the window. Gregory gives up, going back downstairs to spend the evening alone.

It is later in the evening, when he is slumped into the settee, feet up on the coffee table, watching the news, that Ingrid reappears. She loiters in the doorway of the dusk room, lit only by the television blare and a lamp in the corner. Gregory glances up at her. "Feeling better?"

"Yes, a little." She remains in the doorway, her attention flicking between him and the television screen. "Gregory, I have to talk to you."

His hand tightens around the remote control. She sounds quite serious, distinctly worried. This isn't some trivial thing. What is she going to tell him? She never really loved him, only married him to get off the islands. Now that she's got herself set up with work in the city, she wants to get on with the rest of her life. That doesn't include him. Is she going to leave him? He's being melodramatic, but there has always been that inconsistency, how she was in such a rush to marry, before any kind of romantic or physical relationship had really started between them. He's not sure he wants to have this conversation. But perhaps it is nothing. Maybe she is worried about driving lessons; perhaps she wants to increase her hours at work to full time; maybe she's being made redundant.

Ingrid finally braves the room and sits on the settee next to him. She places her hand gingerly on top of his. "Don't be angry."

Gregory closes his eyes. This isn't going to be good. Perhaps she snuck out in the car for a practise drive and pranged it. No, he remembers walking past it when he came home; there was nothing wrong with it. She's going to leave him. He looks over at her. "What is it?"

"I'm pregnant."

He continues to look her directly in the eye, the words somewhere out there, but not quite registering. She's not leaving. She's not saying she never really loved him. What had she said again, or rather, what did that mean?

Ingrid finds her fingers curling around his hand when he doesn't react at all. She is worried. "Say something."

She's pregnant. He starts breathing again. He says the first thing that comes into his mind. "How?"

"How?" Ingrid cracks a smile. "I would have thought you'd have known about that part. It's not exactly been infrequent of late."

Gregory laughs. "No, I don't mean how. I get that." Certainly since moving to Edinburgh the how has been very regular. Ingrid has been quite clingy, most nights seeking him out under the bedclothes before she can get to sleep. "I mean, such as..." He looks at her. How ought she to look? She certainly doesn't look pregnant in any obvious way. "How pregnant are you?"

"About two months. I knew but I thought I would check it with the doctor before I said anything." She looks at him uncertainly. "Is this a good thing?"

Everything happens so quickly with Ingrid. Pregnancy, babies, children. It's not a thing they've spoken of even in first tentative jests. It's not something he's ever particularly brooded over either; he's never felt a desperate need to reproduce, continue the line; certainly seeing how his brother's life has slowly dissolved away to the needs of his three children. Now he is married and his wife is pregnant. But this feels right. Ingrid, and everything that comes with her is what he wants. He breaks into a smile. "Really? We're really pregnant?"

She seems to let her breath go, relieved, and feels her eyes fill up. She moves up closer to him, pressing her forehead against his temple. "Thank God. I was worried you would be angry."

"Ingrid, come on." He drags her into his lap, embracing her. "This is fine. This is a good thing. There'll be you, me, the little screaming one." He dries her eyes with the side of his hand. What was she so worried about? "As long as you don't turn into your mother, there is nothing to get upset over."

Ingrid laughs, kisses him. "I promise. That will never happen."

Gregory is definitely the more nervous of the two. Ingrid is taking this in her stride, as is her surprising way of coping with all kinds of things. Perhaps it is the fact that she has been through so much that makes her hardened to any kind of hospital appointment, any health condition. After all, she has been blind for years. She had brain surgery last year to restore her sight. After those kinds of things, anything must seem possible.

Ingrid is reclining on the hospital bed, unconcerned. The waistband of her trousers is pushed down, her top rolled up to expose her abdomen. Gregory is on a plastic chair beside her, feeling like a spare part. There is a trolley with the ultrasound on beside the bed, and the sonographer is getting a fresh bottle of gel from the cupboard.

"Are we all right this morning?" The sonographer, a second-generation Jamaican with thick black plastic glasses – all the rage at the moment – turns, and looks from Ingrid to Gregory in amusement. The mother looks relaxed, as if she is really for a snooze, whereas the father looks terrified. "This really isn't anything to worry about," she reassures him. "It's just a standard ultrasound, what we call the dating scan. Just to take a look, make sure everything's ok, get a better idea of how old the little one is." She walks over to Ingrid, giving the bottle a quick shake. Gazes down at the woman's exposed stomach and smiles. "Is your other child looking forward to a brother or sister?"

"This is our first," Gregory blurts out.

The woman and Ingrid share a look. "Of course." The sonographer turns away for a moment, before returning to Ingrid. "Just a bit of gel. Bit cold but perfectly harmless. Then we can get started."

The ultrasound goes without any problems. At this stage, at only about two months or so, Ingrid isn't showing, and the baby is tiny, but definitely human looking in form. Reclining in a black hammock that is Ingrid's womb. Alive. A tiny heart beating. His child. In seven month's time this is someone he will hold in his arms.

As is standard behaviour with expectant parents, the ultrasound picture is currently pinned on the fridge, like a postcard from absent friends, shortly due back. Gregory sits and wonders about who this person will become. Every morning over breakfast he looks at the picture and ponders. There are other things to think about. Ingrid is in the kitchen, dressed only in jeans and a vest top. Near the window, on the tips of her toes, stretched up she is trying to put up a curtain hook that has fallen loose from the railings. Her trousers are low-slung and the top is hitched up as she stretches, revealing her midriff. The light moves over her flesh, picking up on marks on the skin. Marks he's always known were there, but has given little thought to, because who of us are really perfect in body, certainly when we've left our teens and the disillusion of adult life hits. These marks that depict the stories of our lives. And he recalls the ultrasound appointment when the sonographer had mistakenly thought that this was not their first child.

Gregory lowers his coffee mug to the kitchen table. "It was funny at the hospital the other day."

"Funny?" Ingrid laughs, just as she manages to catch the curtain hook in place. "You didn't look like you enjoyed going into the hospital."

"Hospitals aren't my favourite places," he admits. "But I meant when that woman was asking about our other child..."

Ingrid rolls back onto her heels.

"As if this wasn't our first."

She lowers her arms, gliding her hands down her hips. Glancing across at him. Smiles. "She probably just thought you looked too old to be having your first baby," she jokes.

"Maybe," he concedes. "Although she was looking at you when she said it."

Ingrid turns back to the window, fingering the open curtains. "Are you saying I look old now?"

"I'd never really thought about the marks on your stomach before. But now that I think over it, I can see why she might have thought they were stretch marks."

Ingrid says nothing.

"It just makes me realise how little I know about you."

"What do you mean by that? You're my husband. You know me. I talk to you."

"But there's things I don't know. When you went for the operation last year, you never told me you were going."

"I didn't want to worry you."

"You think Eilidh broke the news in a sensitive way?"

"I didn't know... there was no guarantee it would be a success. There was always a risk I'd come out a vegetable. I wanted that distance in case something went wrong."

"And then there's your family."

"What about my family?"

"For a family that live so tightly together, you are very dysfunctional. What is that all about?"

"That's just the way we are."

"But something must have started all of this off. You can't tell me things were always like that. If that's so, you couldn't be the person you are; not to come out of something that was never any different."

She shrugs. "Families are just complicated things."

"Complicated." Gregory repeats. "Why did that woman assume this isn't your first child?"

She looks over at him. But says nothing.

"Why did she assume that whilst looking at the stretch marks on your stomach?"

"I don't know," she says quietly.

"Ingrid!" He is surprised by how his voice is suddenly booming. Doubts coming out to the surface. "I am not an idiot. Why did she say that?"

Ingrid looks at the floor.

"Why do I feel like I'm being taken for a fool? Why did you marry me? Was it just to get away from that hell hole you'd call a family home?"

"No, I..."

"So what was it? What has gone on in the past?"

"Why don't you trust me?"

"Trust what? There are all these secrets. Clearly you don't need to tell the fool. I'm just here to serve a purpose. What's the plan? Just stay until you've got yourself set up, then you're off?"

Ingrid can't look him in the eye. She leaves the kitchen, hurrying through to the hallway, pulling her shoes on.

"Where are you going now?"

She picks up her bag, scrabbling with the lock, struggling to get the door open. "I'm leaving."

"You're leaving? And that's it? You won't talk to me; you'll just walk out..."

"Yes."

With that final word, she is gone, the door swinging shut. Silence. Gregory walks through to the kitchen, numbed. He catches sight of the ultrasound picture. His first child. That is the only thing he can be certain of. The only thing except this feeling of been torn apart. She has left him, and all that remains is a grainy printout and an empty home. He's not sure what to do, picks up the mug, but throws it at the cupboard. A loud smash, and streaks as the remaining cold coffee is sprayed out over the kitchen. He sinks to his knees. And feels as though the world has ended.

He remains on the kitchen floor until he notices that the light is starting to fade. It will be night in little over an hour. Ingrid has not come home. Perhaps he will never see her again. Should he have trusted her, or was he right to demand the truth? He doesn't know, only that what is done is done, and he may have managed to destroy his marriage before it is even a year old. His marriage. Too full of gazing longingly at Ingrid to logically, rationally consider how odd the entire affair has been.

Pulling on his jacket, Gregory picks up his keys, and leaves the house. He can't stay indoors anymore. He needs to be away from this, from the streets, the cars, the people, the lights. He needs to be completely alone.

Heading up to the top of his road, he follows the outer road marking the top edge of Duddingston. Here the flowing grass plains mark where Holyrood Park gently begins, patches of trees breaking up the steady green. He follows the road for a short distance, before veering off up the grass, striding through the open space towards the road that circles through Holyrood. Once up on Queen's Drive, he follows the road around the foot of Arthur's Seat, the steep sides and craggy rocks to his right, the vistas out over Edinburgh, Duddingston Loch in the foreground, the sinking sun in the sky. He walks swiftly, trying to pump the anger and the terror out of his veins. Trying to walk it all better. He is angry she has lied, at best refused to talk to him, to tell him what has happened. Refused to trust him. At worst he is distraught. Whatever has happened, whatever her motives were in this marriage, he has come to the point where he does not think he can do without her.

When the road starts to swing back down to the city, away from the more mountainous terrain, towards flat plains and buildings, Gregory jogs up some steps off the tarmac footpath, going onto rough earth tracks. Passing by the gravelled route that goes up along the base of Salisbury Crags, he heads into Hunter's Bog, a dip, a valley in between the regal peak of Arthur's Seat and the steadier climb up to the top of Salisbury Crags. There are good night views to be had from the top of Salisbury Crags, looking out towards the old and new towns of Edinburgh, the castle perched at the top of the Royal Mile, Princess Street in the distance. The edge isn't the safest, especially in the failing light, and the occasional suicide has been known to jump from the top.

He sets up along a vague, barely perceptible path up away from Hunter's Bog, following the long stretched back of Salisbury Crags, an earth covered in rough wild grass and gorse bushes.

He finds her crumpled in the grass by a patch of gorse, quite alone and shivering. She is sobbing heavily, a scene that feels bizarre, and on reflection he can't think that he has ever really seen Ingrid cry. Perhaps it was never the Jameson way. Something bottled up for a long time has been released.

"Ingrid?" He crouches in the grass beside her. She jumps; she's not noticed anyone approaching. Sensitive, perceptive Ingrid is crumbled. She barely senses anything. She almost loses her balance, rolls onto her side, before she leans into him.

"I'm so sorry."

"No, I'm sorry. I shouldn't have lost my temper." He feels her shivering; the temperature is starting to drop. Sitting down on the slopes, he pulls her into him. She still only has the vest top and jeans on, and her bare arms are cool to touch. "I shouldn't force you to confide in me."

"You mustn't think I'm using you," she mumbles, her face pressed up into the curve of his chest. "I know it was all very sudden, but you are the best person I've ever known. I felt safe for..." she coughs, wipes her eyes with the back of her hands and looks at him. "When I came back, after the operation, and went back to the farm, I just couldn't stay there. I had to get away. It's so big out here, and so lonely. I know I was being impulsive when I asked you to marry me, but I had to try. It was the only thing I could think that I wanted."

She shuffles around, so that her back is against his chest, and they sit together above Hunter's Bog, watching the light disappear in silence. It is a cold, cloudless night, and already light from the moon is giving some faded definition.

"You don't regret it?"

"Regret?"

"Marrying me."

He puts his face in her hair, breathing in her scent. "No."

"Knowledge changes things. How you see people..."

He is not sure that he wants to know any more. There is something in the tone of her voice. Something about the atmosphere of the Jameson farm. Bad things happened there.

"Not talking hasn't helped me," she continues, grateful for the darkness. She won't be able to see the look on his face. "I lost my sight when I was ten. It was very sudden, over night. Terrifying. It took a lot of time to get used to. I decided to stop talking when I was fourteen. That was when I pretended I was deaf. I didn't want to communicate with the world. And then suddenly I find I'm thirty; I've missed out on all of my twenties. I'm still stuck in my own prison, and nothing has gotten better. It hadn't solved anything. And then you came to the farm. And I thought maybe it would be worth the risk having the operation."

"I can only begin to imagine how difficult it was losing your sight. You were angry that it was just you. You stopped talking..."

"It wasn't because of that." Ingrid closes her eyes. She hasn't spoken of this, either in words or sign language, to anyone. Everything, this, every other thought and emotion has been bottled up all these years because she did not wish to lower herself to deal with the world again. This tactic hasn't worked; hasn't brought her what she wanted. It is time to bring things to a close.

"I became pregnant when I was thirteen."

Gregory closes his eyes, feels his heart break a little. The stretch marks.

"My mother..." her voice wavers. "Is a Catholic. My father was brought up to believe that certain... practices were not acceptable. Abortion wasn't... it just wasn't an option. Despite the circumstances. I was raped..."

Oh Jesus. He folds his arms around her.

"So it wasn't exactly planned. But they made me go through with it, with the pregnancy. I spoke less and less, and after the birth I just stopped. I didn't listen anymore. I just existed."

He knows he does not want to ask this question, to hear confirmation of what he now suspects, but he cannot help himself. "What happened to the baby?"

"We're quite insular. Isolated. It's in our nature. Keep it in the family." Her voice is bitter. "It wasn't my choice."

"Shea?"

Ingrid bites her lip. It will be the first time she's acknowledged this, ever since that first moment, the first cry.

"Does she...?"

"No," she says quickly. "My mother dealt with that. She thinks we're sisters. I know my mother is very cold; she's a difficult woman to like, but she's very strong. She took over immediately."

"She shouldn't have made you go through with it."

"What's done is done," Ingrid whispers. She twists to look at him, but it is difficult to read his expression in this poor light. Sight hasn't been the system she's relied on for a long time. Even though her eyes are open and seeing every day she still relies on other senses to read people. She touches the side of his face. "You're not going to leave me?"

"Leave you?" He suppresses a laugh. This isn't the time, but it seems ridiculous that she should ask him that when it is the very thing he has feared. "No. I am going to take you home." He stands up, pulling her to her feet. "Thank you for telling me."

Shrugging off his jacket, he puts it around his wife's shoulders as he looks across the landscape of long dark shadows in Hunter's Bog. "It's just question of how we're going to get back down without breaking our legs."

Ingrid grips his hand. "Lucky for you, you married an expert at walking blind."

Five months. Almost to the day. Four more months, then nothing will be the same. Gregory has spent the summer clearing out the spare room – filled with clutter he has never bothered to sort through since moving into the house. Most of it is simply rearranged to the loft to be dealt with properly some day in the future. A little is properly unpacked, and a couple of things are thrown out. The spare room is now clear in preparation for the baby. He has started back at work, colleagues joking that he won't know what hit him. His life will never be his own again.

It is the early evening. Ingrid returned from work an hour ago, and has retreated upstairs for a nap. She is tired, commenting that she has never been so tired. The pregnancy is taking all kinds of effects on her body. Technically she has been here before, her body knows what to expect. But in many respects she treats this as her first child. This is the first that is wanted, that she is looking forward to. The true first, the episode back home, is never spoken of. It is no longer a secret between them, but Ingrid prefers to pretend it never happened, a feat that is much easier now she is living in Edinburgh. The question over the sense of ignoring the great elephant is academic in any case, as Gregory wouldn't know what to say about it had they chosen to talk. He only knows that he is horrified by what her parents forced her to go through with all those years ago.

He is sitting at the kitchen table, flicking through an advanced proof copy of the new Shetland guidebook. He looks at what changes the editor has made; whether all his maps have been used or if the publishing house has adapted his work a lot. It is a comprehensive book, covering everything necessary for a holiday. They just need to drum up interest in the Shetlands as a bigger component of the Scotland experience to build the market for the book.

The phone starts ringing. He glances across the table, where the cordless phone rests on top of an unopened bag of apples. Probably just a sales call, but he answers anyway. "Hello?"

There is a pause on the line. "Mr Hughson?"

Anyone who starts a telephone call with him so formally at this time in the evening is usually trying to sell something; but that Irish voice is too familiar. He is surprised to hear from her; even more so as he realises that they've not had a single call since they moved back to Edinburgh. He wonders if Ingrid has even told her she is pregnant. "Eilidh," he responds. "Are we going to be formal when we're family now?"

"Family," Eilidh mutters as if the notion is a joke.

She's clearly not changed, he thinks, raising his eyes to the ceiling. "Ingrid's taking a nap at the moment..."

"No matter," Eilidh interrupts him. "You can take a message. It'll probably be better coming from you anyway."

News. Of course it must be news for Eilidh to ring. Either that or an urgent request. She has never struck him as the kind of woman who enjoys idle chit chat.

"I'll cut to the chase," she tells him, as if she is the kind of woman who does anything but. "John died two days ago."

"Jesus," Gregory blurts out without thinking. Old John Jameson, not really that old these days, in his late sixties. Quiet, few on words, hard working. Trying to keep a farm together with little money. He remembers the packet of cash John had given him for Ingrid for the wedding. The only real token for the occasion from the family, which Gregory managed to get Ingrid to spend on herself eventually. And yet a man who forced his young daughter to go through with a pregnancy that has clearly brought nothing but misery on the family since. Dead. It feels incomprehensible. "I'm so sorry..."

Eilidh draws in her breath. Gregory wonders if this has affected her in anyway. She was always the iron woman, cold, ultra-independent, and yet even Eilidh must have feelings. There is no weeping, and no sense of loss. Just the simple plain facts.

"How did he...?"

"It was a heart attack, he died of sudden cardiac arrest," she says, very matter of fact. "It would have been very quick, over in the blink of an eye. He was at work; I found him in one of the fields. I'm calling to let you know the funeral is next week. Tuesday morning at ten o'clock at the Lunna Kirk."

"I should go wake Ingrid."

"No, leave her be," Eilidh tells him. "You'll do better at telling her. I just needed to get the message through. I'll perhaps see you both next week."

"Yes, of course."

"Goodbye, then."

"Bye..."

She has already hung up. Gregory hangs up the phone and sets it down on the table. John Jameson died two days ago, yet she has only contacted them this evening. He thinks of Ingrid resting upstairs. He will have to tell her when she comes down for something to eat. He has no idea how she'll react.

This is the second time he is wearing a suit on Shetland. He might have made some comment that the first was in happy circumstances; the second being quite the opposite. But he is not sure if he can class this as a sad occasion, for there are no tears shed. People deal with grief and loss in very different ways, but Gregory has to admit that this is the strangest funeral, as far as the atmosphere goes, that he has ever been to.

On the face of it, it is an average funeral, held in the local church, mourners dressed in black. It is a small gathering: the widow and *daughters* of various meanings of the term; a few locals and the one son in law. He hasn't seen Andrew, but a couple of people did enter the church after them, so perhaps Andrew is hiding in the background. Ingrid and Eilidh are sitting at the front, both in black dresses, with expressions like wax figurines. For a family that is so estranged from one another, these two women seem to pull the most strength from one another, and Gregory senses a solidarity, the closest thing to love that could exist in the Jameson clan. Shea is sat close by on the same pew, but seems separated. Her arms are folded and she looks more seven than her seventeen years, a sulking child who doesn't see why she should have to be here.

It is a sparse gathering. The church has a small interior and for regular funerals probably wouldn't hold everyone who wanted to come. Today it feels embarrassingly empty. Has John Jameson's passing meant so little to the world? They should have invited the sheep along; Gregory suspects they will be the ones who miss him most, now that there is no shepherd to care for them. Other than close (as in blood ties) family, a few locals have turned up, possibly more out of an allegiance to community spirit than any real feeling of loss. Gregory has noted Miriam Rea from the Lunna Guesthouse; Calum Moran, the salmon farmer and evening fiddle maestro; Jayne and Hugo Castleton – Jayne slimmer now that the baby has been born; David Henriksson from Lerwick, and a couple of other faces that are familiar but he cannot recall the names of.

The Lunna Kirk is a small white rectangular building just down the hill from the Lunna Guest House. Surrounded by its own walled churchyard, it offers some protection from the sea winds. Today, as they file out of the church, this defence does not feel comforting. The sky is grey and the winds are picking up. A heavy rainstorm has been forecast for later in the day.

The vicar leads the way around behind the church to the dank hole the gravediggers prepared the previous day. The coffin is carried by funeral staff and taken to the graveside. The close family stand nearest, but Shea, either overwhelmed or bored, shuffles away to loiter in amongst the locals as if this has nothing to do with her. Gregory notices Andrew stood further away, back towards the kirk, beside the dark grey stone steps leading to a first floor entrance at one end of the building. Gregory raises a hand slightly, whether to acknowledge his presence or encourage him to join the rest of the family, he's not sure. Andrew gives a barely perceptible nod of the head, but makes no move to join the funeral procession. Perhaps this death has hit him worst of all, Gregory thinks. Andrew has been so adamant in not coming back to Shetland; now that his father has passed on, perhaps he is riddled with guilt over how little he valued his family. He stands like a sentry, or a gravedigger waiting to finish the work, in a black overcoat, hands dug into the pockets, lank hair blowing in the wind.

The vicar is still droning. It has been a heavy, religious and distinctly depressive ceremony. There is much talk of the Lord, of how this is how we will all go in the end, and we can only hope and pray that we will ascend, and not descend in a pit of sin, to be tortured by devils.

"Ashes to ashes..."

Funk to funky, Gregory thinks of David Bowie's famous song. Inappropriate thoughts at a funeral. He suppresses a smile – not that it is amusing, rather that sometimes in such serious situations the body tries to rebel and provoke the most inappropriate responses.

The coffin has been lowered into the ground. The vicar closes his prayer book, to signal he has finished. He solemnly gestures to Eilidh, stepping back from the head of the grave. Time to pass by and say goodbye. John Jameson has really gone, and his remains are now replanted in this land he came from, lived and breathed.

Eilidh walks up to the head of the grave, her face taught and expressionless. She takes a handful of soil from the heap at the side, and throws it into the grave. The first scattering of earth to keep John in his place. Up until now everything has been as expected, if a little emotionless. But this is a Jameson funeral, and something is bound to happen. Expression and thoughts filter across her eyes, and a scowl builds on her face. Her lips pucker and she spits into the grave, in any other circumstance a distance and direction that would have made any schoolboy proud. Here it is sacrilege. There is a sharp intake of horrified breath across the non-family members, and yet no one dares say anything. They are all trying their best to pretend they didn't just see.

The widow steps away from the grave and heads back towards the church. There is no second glance back to the grave. He is dead and she is moving on. Ingrid follows, now a good five months pregnant with a noticeable bump. She follows suit in taking a handful of soil and throwing it gently into the hole. She hovers, then makes to move and Gregory thinks this is the end of it, but she follows suit and also spits into the grave. This provokes an even more horrified response from the gathering, and Gregory finds himself looking across at the locals he has spent more time with than Ingrid's family, looking for some reassurance that it did just happen, it wasn't his imagination, and that it was indeed shocking.

People are ready to file by and get back into the warmth of the Lunna Guest House for the repost. Gregory is at the head of the grave and wonders if this bizarre behaviour is some kind of family ritual that he will be expected to partake in. He bears John Jameson no ill will, and wonders where the hate has come from to carry such furry beyond his death. He knows from what Ingrid has told him, that both John and Eilidh made her go through with the pregnancy when she was raped, and as a result she locked herself away on the farm, in her own self for over fifteen years as a kind of punishment on them all. But he had thought she was trying to give up that and move on. Live the rest of her life in some happiness. Grief does strange things to people, and perhaps John's death has brought all those feelings back up, raw and stabbing, as if it only happened last week.

The fire is crackling and the lights are on in the Lunna Guesthouse, warm and welcoming. A stark contrast from outside. The atmosphere is subdued, locals present out of a sense of duty outnumbering family members and mourners. Eilidh has paid for this spread, but does not care to stay, and as soon as everyone has had chance to pass on their condolences to her, she is away back to the farm. Shea sits at the corner of the bar, with a pint in front of her even though she is underage. Today no one is going to stop her. Ingrid looks tired, and is already across the room at one of the cushioned seats near the fire. Jayne Castleton has tentatively approached; having never spoken to her before even though they have been neighbours for decades, and starts up a conversation on babies; something reasonably inoffensive and a little common ground as one has given birth in the last few months, the other due in the future. Like everyone else, they are avoiding the giant white elephant in the room and not speaking of the dead, or what just happened out in the graveyard.

Gregory still feels numb. In a lot of ways he is not surprised by Eilidh – social niceties are of no concern to her. But Ingrid seemed to him more sensitive, especially these days with her hormones on overdrive; she will sit at cry at the slightest prompting from the television. Yet he has still to see her loose one tear over the death of her father.

He approaches the bar, the opposite end, as short as it is, to Shea, where Calum and David stand, talking to Miriam. They look around as Gregory approaches, Miriam's eyes wide. "Honest to God, Gregory," she starts, her voice low. "Do you know what all that was about?"

"I don't know," Gregory starts, as Calum pours him a whisky from the bottle on the bar. "It's not a local tradition then?"

Calum snorts. "Not a Shetland way in any case."

"Bloody weird," David agrees.

"It's good to see you here," Gregory tells him. "There doesn't seem to be that many turned up."

"Aye, well," David sighs. "I gave Andrew a lift up."

Andrew, of course. Gregory scans over the room, but he can't see him. "Has he not come back?"

David shakes his head. "He's been very strange on this visit, even for Andrew. Said he couldn't face coming in. Anyway, he'd already arranged for some lassie to come and pick him up. He's waiting outside for her." He glances at his watch. "Any time now; they're probably already away."

"Andrew's seeing a local lass now?" Miriam asks.

"Seeing and seeing," David says. "He's not changed. "Some lass he met last time he was here, Sharon something or other. I don't know how he does it. I think he was chasing her friend on the last visit. He's only been here a day and a half or so and he's already got his lodgings with her sorted out. Parents are away so she has the house to herself."

"Christ, she's not a teenager is she?"

"Ack, no, she's in her early twenties, just still living at home. But you know what Andrew was like, is like. He'll no change now."

"Is he staying near here?"

"No, he's down at Troswickness, near Dunrossness and Bodam," David says. "Down Sumburgh way," he adds for Gregory's benefit, a little unnecessary as Gregory is quite familiar with the geography of the islands, having spent several months exploring them in great detail. "Away down one of the wee roads towards the coast. Nice sea views apparently."

Someone touches Gregory's elbow, and he turns away, surprised to see Ingrid there. "Would it be ok if we took a break and went up to the farm?"

She sounds apologetic, as if she is causing an inconvenience. This is a day when she can ask for whatever she wishes.

"I just wanted to speak to my mother," she continues, "Before she goes. I think she's flying out to Ireland this evening."

"Sure." Gregory puts his glass down. He's only drunk half the whisky. "We'll be back in a bit," he tells the others, who reciprocate with mutterings of agreements and vague pleasantries; all the while wishing to ask Ingrid what the spitting was about, but not daring to bring the matter up.

They walk out of the guesthouse and back down the road to the kirk. The hire car is parked just by the entrance to the churchyard. There hadn't seemed much point in driving up to the guesthouse's small park, only a couple of hundred metres away, and Ingrid is still quite adamant that she is capable of everything, to the same degree as she was before she became pregnant.

Gregory glances across at her as he starts the engine. "Are you all right?"

"Sure." She pulls her seatbelt on.

She's not going to explain the dramatics in the graveyard unless you ask, Gregory thinks. He's not sure how far he dare push the issue. "It's just that the burial..."

"Is over," Ingrid finishes for him.

"You're not angry with your father?"

"Not anymore."

They drive up past the guesthouse and down the road, an old familiar route that Gregory hasn't touched for months. Nothing has changed; it's as if they never were away.

"Could we see the cottage?" Ingrid asks as they near the pull off for Gregory's old crofter's cottage. "Just one last time?"

It is starting to spot with rain as Gregory pulls the car up outside his old home and turns off the engine. Ingrid is the first to step outside into the chilly autumnal air. She hurries to the back of the car, opening the boot and pulling out her waterproof coat to put on over her black formal jacket. The boot lid slams back down in place as Gregory gets out of the car.

The front door isn't locked. Inside the air is stale, on pause, and the atmosphere is damp and chilly. The stop tap was turned on, but there is a build up of moisture. The fireplace is black and cold. It is bare of human habitation, even more so than the sparse home Gregory had set up for himself. The bed box, now empty of bedding and body heat, is just a musty old antique. Gregory stands at the window and listens to the drizzle patter against the window. Ingrid steps into the room, and he looks over at her. "Shall we go up to the farm?" He is keen to get this over with.

"Let's walk."

"It's raining. I don't think..."

"We have our jackets," she interrupts, quite sure he was about to tell her that she shouldn't walk in the rain in her condition. "It's not far. I'm not sure when I'll next be here. I'd like to get all my unfinished business sorted out, loose ends tied up."

So they walk through the fields up to the farm, Gregory glad that she had been complaining of swollen ankles and had put on a pair of trainers this morning. The farmyard feels empty, finished, upon approach. Even though John was rarely seen, his absence is noticeable. The wind blows through, hollow, dead and grey. It suddenly feels like they truly are at the ends of the earth.

"I think I might go up and take a look around my old flat."

The last of Ingrid's personal possessions were packed up and either shipped out to Edinburgh or sold months ago. There won't be much to see, just an empty unlived in flat, but he can understand that she might want to take a final look. He can't imagine that they will be coming back to the Jameson farm for happy holidays and merry family reunions. She spent so much time here; it has been a big part of her life, as much as she may regret some of the choices she took. It is as she said; she is getting the loose ends tied up. Saying goodbye to the place.

"All right, we can go up and take a look around."

Ingrid stays him, a hand to his forearm. "I'd like to go up on my own."

The wind blows through him. He looks over to the main building, where the front door is half open. "I'll go wait in the kitchen."

Ingrid heads up the stairs to her little flat. Gregory, feeling mildly rejected, treads across to the farmhouse. It's very quiet, not even the old sheepdog, Seamus, is loitering at the sidelines. Pushing open the door a little wider, he steps into the front entrance and out of the wind. There are voices in the kitchen, Eilidh and Shea, and he almost walks in until he realises they are talking about him and Ingrid. He falters, and quietly sits down on a bench in the hall running along the kitchen wall. He is tired, and has no more energy for Ingrid's family.

"I still can't believe she married him," Shea trunters. "He's so old."

"Ingrid's in her thirties. There's not that much between them."

"Well, she barely knew him."

There is the sound of an object being set down. "And what kind of time frame do you think is decent before someone does something major like that? Getting married, hopping into someone's bed?"

Shea doesn't have an answer for this, just a sigh that pours out of the back of her throat.

"Anyway, we have some things to sort out," Eilidh continues. "This is for you."

"An envelope?" Shea sounds less than impressed.

"They're all the keys for the flat in Lerwick."

"I already have a key," she says, her tone of voice patronising as if Eilidh is simple minded.

"You never did listen, did you, girl? I said they're all the keys for the flat. You're almost eighteen; you'll be needing somewhere to live and you can't stay here."

"I don't want to share the flat with you."

"You won't. I've signed it across to you. You are the sole owner."

Silence. Shea is uncertain at this news. "Where are you going to stay when you're working at the hospital?"

"I won't; I've handed my notice in."

"Handed your notice in? You're changing jobs? Or are you just going to sit up here and rot?"

"No such thing. I'm away back to Ireland."

"What, for a holiday?"

"For good."

And perhaps if they'd left it there, things could have ended on a relatively neutral key. But Shea cannot let things go. She is always looking to pick a fight. "You're just leaving, for good, like that? And what about me? I'm just going to live in Lerwick completely on my own. Pa's dead, Andrew and Ingrid have fucked off to the mainland and now you're away back to the old country? What kind of a mother are you?"

"Not yours."

"You never wanted me."

"Your mother gave up on you the moment you were conceived, and that's why you got me." Eilidh's voice is terse, even for her. Things that have been bottled up for so many years are coming loose, and once the flow has been started, perhaps it will never be stopped.

Shea laughs. "What, you want to tell me that I'm adopted?"

Don't push it, Gregory thinks.

"No, only that your own mother rejected you and I had to raise you. I have the misfortune of being your grandmother."

A chair scraps across the stone flagstones in the kitchen. "What the fuck are you saying?"

"Don't use language like that with me."

"But if you're not my mother, who is? Oh my God," she gasps. It's hard to tell if she's weeping. "Ingrid? You're saying Ingrid's actually my mother?" She coughs, gargling on her own words. She is definitely crying now. "Why didn't you just leave me with Ingrid?"

"She didn't want you."

"She would have. She would have been better than you."

"I think I did a good job considering you should have come out with a curly tail."

Gregory feels a weight plummet in his stomach, like a stone being dropped from a great height. He closes his eyes. From the way Shea continues to shout, it seems that she has missed what Eilidh is alluding to. It is probably enough for today to learn that Ingrid is actually her mother and not her sister. Perhaps months from now, she will go through this conversation again, and realise what had been said. For now, Eilidh is not her real mother, and she is being abandoned to the world to look after herself, completely unwanted. It doesn't seem to be a great difference to the rest of her life up until this moment, only that now it is spelt out to her.

Sobbing loudly, Shea runs out of the kitchen, too upset to notice Gregory in the hallway. She flees the farmhouse, scrambling on to her little scooter – a new addition since Gregory was here last – and rides out of the farmyard.

Gregory remains. Curly tails. Spitting in the grave. Why did mother and daughter hate him so much? He listens to Eilidh stomp around in the kitchen; clearly Shea has managed to annoy her, as much as she would never admit it.

The misery and the abuse, which must have soaked into the very fabric of this place over the decades, feels stiflingly oppressive. It's no wonder Ingrid stopped talking, played deaf and switched off final lines of communication. When she had needed to be heard, no rescue had come, so why bother after that?

He stands and walks to the kitchen doorway. Eilidh is surrounded by packing boxes, the kitchen like the crofter's cottage, emptied and no longer lived in. She must have worked fast to have reached this stage already. Some old newspapers are opened out on the kitchen table, as the final items are packed up. She has a small glass vase in her hands as he makes his presence known.

"I suppose you were listening in on all that." Eilidh says.

There's no point in pretending. "Yes."

"There's one or two things about your new wife you never knew."

"I already knew Shea is her daughter."

Eilidh looks up sharply, genuinely surprised. "Well, perhaps this thing between you and Ingrid is more genuine than I first thought," she comments. "If she's told you."

"She never mentioned the part about being raped by her own father."

The vase smashes on the floor. "Don't you dare."

"You're going to defend a dead man who abused your daughter?"

"John Jameson may have made a lot of mistakes," she roars at him, her face taking on a pinkish tinge of fury. "But he never laid a finger on his children, neither of them, and don't you ever forget that."

"I understood what you meant by curly tails, even if Shea didn't."

Eilidh stares steadily at him.

Gregory feels his confidence falter a little. "You both spat in his grave."

She says nothing.

Oh Jesus. Gregory steps into the room, pulling a chair away from the table. Perhaps it ought to have been obvious. Something terrible had happened here, but it wasn't the horror rather the guilt that created the distance.

"Ingrid lost her sight when she was ten. She didn't stop talking and hearing until she was fourteen, well, until Shea had been born. I suppose she'd given up on the lot of us by then, and I can't blame her." Eilidh sat at the table, opposite Gregory. They could look at one another through a corridor of boxes. "Losing her sight made her very vulnerable. It took her a long time to get used to the world without sight. And I suppose her not being able to look at people made it easier for him..." she stops. "I didn't know; we didn't know what was happening until I realised Ingrid was pregnant. Then it all came out. It had been going on for months, well over a year. And when we found out, when we could put a stop to it, it was too late."

Gregory is furious. On behalf of the child Ingrid, the Ingrid today. That this abuse could have happened, and that she has been left to live in the prison it created ever since. "As far as I can tell, Andrew's never been punished for this."

"John idolised that boy. He loved all... he loves, well, loved, he's passed on now." Eilidh shakes her head to herself. Perhaps she is not as settled with his passing as she thought. She raises her head, looks Gregory in the eye. It's all very well being moral and righteous in hindsight and impartiality. It's not so easy when you're in the heat of the moment. "Where I come from, abortion is a sin. A mortal sin, no exceptions. You'll go to hell. I was very certain of my beliefs back then. But now, after all I've seen, not just with Ingrid. I'm a midwife; I see all kinds of domestic situations. And I just don't know if it's right to be forever bringing new people into unhappy homes where they're not wanted. That a foetus' rights always override those that are already out here, born, living their lives. Or trying to. As if all we're here for is procreation, and nothing else matters. Nothing at all.

She pauses. "John's very family orientated. There was no way that baby was ever going to leave the family. So I became mother. He just didn't have it in him to punish the boy, or hand him over to the authorities, admit what had happened. We kept them apart as much as we could. I have a flat in Lerwick; it's easier when I work night shifts at the hospital. Andrew stayed there more and more. And when he was eighteen he was away to the mainland and he's barely been back since."

"I did wonder why he never came to visit Ingrid in Edinburgh."

"Oh, he never wanted to be anywhere near her after we found out. Especially now that she'll be able to look at him again." She entwines her fingers together. "Where is Ingrid?"

"She's in the flat. I'll go get her." Gregory leaves the farmhouse. Outside it is raining heavily. The clouds hang low, grey and dense. This has set in for the rest of the day. He hurries across the yard and up the staircase. Dripping, he enters the flat. "Ingrid?"

It is empty. He checks the bathroom, then circles in the flat again. Where is she?

He runs back to the farmhouse. "Has she come in just now?" he asks Eilidh, but already he knows the answer. "Maybe she went back to the cottage."

"You walked over from the cottage?"

"Yes, I left the car there." He touches his jacket pocket. It feels empty. He checks his pockets, coat, jacket, trousers. There is no car key. "Shit." Leaving Eilidh with no other goodbye, he runs back out into the rain, and starts across the fields towards the little cottage. He is not surprised when he staggers up to the door, breathing heavily, to see that the car has gone. Ingrid has driven away without telling him. There are ugly suggestions in his mind as to what she might be doing. Groaning, he pushes himself away from the prop of the wall, and starts jogging again, heading for the road and Lunna Guesthouse.

The wipers on David Henriksson's car are going at the fastest speed. The rainstorm appears to be hitting a peak of intensity, and the rain pours over his windscreen as if he is driving through a car wash. The noise of the rainfall drumming on the roof of his car is tremendous. He cannot drive particularly fast, which he is aware is annoying Gregory, but with visibility as it is, the road still single lane until they near the Laxo ferry terminal, and him having had a couple of drinks, he has no intention of risking his car or his health for something that may turn into nothing. It will be a good hour and a half's drive, and he wonders how Gregory will cope with the wait.

He is still not sure what exactly is going on. Gregory had staggered back into the bar about half an hour ago, his rain coat flapping open, his hair soaked, and gasping for breath as if he had just run a marathon. Everyone's immediate thought was that there had been an accident and they needed to call an ambulance, but apparently no one was hurt. Gregory had gone directly to David and asked if he had his car here – of course, he'd given Andrew a lift up to the funeral. The lassie Andrew was staying with hadn't been able to drive him to the funeral as her shift wouldn't finish in time.

Gregory had then asked him to drive him to Andrew, Dunrossness, wasn't it? David didn't have a problem with this; it would get him away from the funeral party, but didn't Gregory have his own car? Ingrid had taken it. He thought Ingrid had taken it to go and see Andrew.

David still doesn't understand why there is a panic on. If Ingrid wants to go and see her brother, what is the problem? But Gregory looks ill with worry, and he couldn't say no to the man. So here they are, driving along in the thrashing rain on a wild goose chase.

Gregory is slumped in the passenger seat, impatiently drumming his fingers at the base of the window. It will be a long drive with little talking. He knows that David thinks he is being irrational, and perhaps he is right. There is no real reason, nothing concrete at least, to panic over. Only that he has a bad sense of foreboding, and the very fact that Ingrid has clearly sneaked away, trying to strand him up at the farm where he is out of reach to hinder her does nothing to calm his nerves. He could try to explain it to David, the fact that Andrew and Ingrid have had nothing to do with one another for eighteen years for very good reason, but this is a family secret that most certainly is not his to disclose. Even though Ingrid is the victim, a vulnerable blind girl at the time, to know that she had been raped by her own brother would change the way people looked at her, regarded her. And this is something she has to live with.

They take a turn off from the main road towards Scalloway, cutting across the island to follow the A970 along an easy run down the eastern coastline. Everything is grey, dark and damp, the landscape cut up by the pounding rain. The occasional set of headlights going in the opposite direction cut through the air. They are heading towards Sumburgh, and the altitude is dropping, the land starting to flatten out. David turns off the main road at a junction marked for Troswickness and Bodam, immediately back on to single lane roads.

"And you're sure Andrew's staying down here?"

"Yes," David says as he takes a turning to the left in the scattered village of Bodam. The next road feels even more like a little track heading to a lonely farm. It is a shame the weather is so poor, because this patch is especially idyllic in the sunshine, like a

Shetland holiday coast with turquoise sea waters, green fields and flat plains. "Are you sure this is where she'll be?"

"I hope not," Gregory mutters.

"You hope not?" Why have they driven all this way in that case?

The road swings back on itself, following the edge of the coastline to go in an eventual loop back up to the main road. Gregory leans forward, pulling against his seatbelt. They are approaching a small, modern build estate to the left, and there is a car poorly parked on the side of the junction. It is half on the grass, the bonnet only just centimetres away from colliding with the street sign. "There." He points to it as if David is incapable of seeing what is right in front of him. "That's the hire car."

David drives past the car and pulls up onto the footpath on the opposite side of the road to where Ingrid has parked. He turns off the car engine, and they are enveloped by the sound of the rain.

"Do you know which house it is?"

David shakes his head. "Just somewhere on this road."

Gregory is out of the car. Pulling up the hood of his coat, he hurries over to the hire car, rather pointlessly, because he can already see it is empty. He tries the door, but it is locked. Now what? He looks up the road, the collection of modern houses and bungalows. Will he have to go door to door?

"Excuse me!" An elderly woman is in the doorway of the house on the junction corner. She has an umbrella opened and is walking down the pathway to the front gate where Gregory is. "Are you looking for the lass who left her car there?"

"Yes."

"Red-haired lass."

"Yes, that's my wife. Please, can you tell me where she's gone?"

"She went up to the Ryan's house. It's not the day to be running about outdoors, I can tell you. Rain like we've not had for a good few months..."

She probably lives alone, sits by the window and watches the comings and goings of her neighbours. A new person to talk to, ramble on about nothing. Gregory doesn't have the time for this. "Which one is the Ryan's house?"

She points up the road. "The peach coloured house just there you see, with the red roof."

"Thank you."

Gregory jogs up towards the bungalow, aware of David begrudgingly following on behind. The front door is around the far side of the property. It looks like a permanent residence, a family home. There is a car parked out the front, tubs of drowned flowers that look as though they've been touched by the frost and will be dead soon. Please let her be in here, Gregory thinks, as he hammers on the front door.

Footsteps hurry towards the door, it is flung open and a young woman, barely out of her teens, muddy blonde hair tied scruffily up, wearing a sweater and jeans that pinch at her hips. Gregory stares at her for a moment; she is familiar but he can't quite place her. "Who are you?"

She is at first disappointed that a stranger is calling; she had obviously been expecting someone else. Her expression soon changes to irritation at his question. It has been a strange day, and she has just about had enough of people. "Sharon Ryan. Why, who are you?"

"Gregory Hughson. Look, is my wife here, Ingrid?"

"Who?"

"What about Andrew Jameson?"

"Andrew?" This is immediately a name in common. "He's out. Some weird pregnant woman turned up a while ago."

"Ingrid."

"Was that Ingrid?" She doesn't sound interested, in fact if anything she sounds resentful and jealous. "I don't know. I thought maybe she was Andrew's wife or something, the way he freaked out. He told me he was single, but that never means anything, does it."

"Where are they?"

"Off up there." She waves her arm vaguely out in the rain.

"Can you show me?"

"It's raining."

"Please, it's important."

She sighs in exasperation. As she takes her coat down from the hooks by the door, David appears beside Gregory. From her expression, she obviously recognises him. "David, isn't it? What are you doing here?"

"Looking for Andrew."

She looks from David and back to Gregory. "I remember you," she exclaims, examining Gregory more closely. "You were over here a couple of years ago or something. At the Lounge in Lerwick. Me and Hafdis were playing. You were there with Andrew."

He remembers now. The two girls playing the fiddles. Sharon had been the rejected girl, Andrew going for the exotic instead; the Norwegian friend.

Sharon steps out into the rain, pulling the door to. "They just went walking away over here," she explains as she goes further up the road. "Not really out for a stroll, Andrew was on his own and she was following him. I don't think he wanted to talk to her."

They walk up through the little estate, past houses and fenced off patches of grass. These must be new builds, because the gardens are little more than the grass that was already there before the properties were built. The occasional swing set has been put up for the children, but that is all. No trees, no shrubs, no flowers in the ground – the usual features of an established garden. The road swings up and around to the left, ending with a turning space lined by six white fronted garages in a terrace. Beyond this there is gently rising rough grassland, at the height of what they can see, a dry stone wall running along a boundary. The intensity of the rain starts to pick up again. Sharon wipes the rainwater from her eyes and points over the tops of the garages. "Can you see the walls up there?"

The rise is a little steeper in that direction. Gregory squints into the rain. It is difficult to make out in this visibility, especially as this is new to him, but he thinks he can make out the walls, a gap in the boundary. Beyond this wall there is another dumpy rise with some kind of wall or derelict building around it.

"They went walking up through there."

"In this rain?" David sounds baffled. He has pulled up his collar and is holding it forward to stop the rain tumbling down the back of his neck. Neither he nor Sharon have hoods on their jackets. "Why would they go up there? What's to see?"

"Not much. Just grass and a wee pond," Sharon admits. "But you can't get far, because you're soon on the cliffs."

Gregory feels sick. "The cliffs?"

"They're quite dramatic."

It's just another way of saying dangerous, he thinks. Slowly closing his eyes. If Ingrid was clearing up all her business on Shetland, what kind of business does she need to deal with at the top of a sea cliff in a storm?

"I think they're coming back," David says.

Gregory opens his eyes. There is a single, lone figure at the side of the hillock, cresting over the top and heading for the gap in the wall. The coat they are wearing gives them a boxy look. They are hunched over against the weather, and at this distance and in this visibility they are little more than a shape. They are not walking particularly fast, for they are no longer in any hurry. There is a sense of relaxation, or relief, as if this is all finally over. Previous attempts to ignore it, to punish, to guilt trip or to run away have not worked. The past eighteen years have proved that. But it is time to move on properly, and this has now finally resolved the nightmare. Gregory watches the slow progress and cannot say whether it is Ingrid or Andrew. He squints through the torrents, trying to get a sharper image. It's not possible.

"But there's only one person," Sharon looks around at Gregory, now most definitely her age, white-faced and looking for reassurance from the adults. Reassurance no one is able to give. She is correct; there is only one person, Ingrid or Andrew coming back from the cliffs. As of yet it is impossible to say which.

A Note

I don't speak Irish Gaelic, so undoubtedly any errors or crudeness of language in the few sentences that appear in the story are a result of my internet-based translations. I hope these can be forgiven.

The story itself is a work of pure fiction, and all events and characters are entirely products of my imagination. Any resemblance is completely coincidental.

Although Gregory's tourist book does not exist, the Shetland Islands do, and are most definitely worth the visit.